ALPH

✳ ✳ ✳

To my buddy Jack

Lee

BY LEE CARSON

ISBN: 1494402416
ISBN 13: 9781494402419
Library of Congress Control Number: 2013922504
CreateSpace Independent Publishing Platform
North Charleston, South Carolina

Lee

I want to thank you for sharing *"Alph"* with me.

I must tell you the truth: that after I read the cast of characters and prologue to the story, I made the mistake of thinking that this story might turn out to be a little slow and of mild interest to me. Thanks for proving me so wrong in my presumption.

You have a talent in your writing skills that I do envy. In a few lines, up to a single paragraph, you can define a character (or a donkey) completely. As the story progresses, the growth of each character expands.

I read the entire story in a day. I enjoyed it immensely.

This is a story for young children, adults and senior adults. We all can glimpse a character that is, or was a friend or relative we knew.

Please get this story published. I feel that I have looked back in time and glimpsed a people and life that existed at the very beginning of Christianity, and this is something that is needed today and tomorrow.

God bless you.
Your church family brother,
Joe Maxwell

This book is dedicated to my grandchildren
whom I dearly love.

Megan Carson, Haley Metzner, and grand-son-in-law
Paul Metzner

Lee Carson is a retired vocational teacher who taught for forty-five years. He has also taught children and youth Sunday school classes most of his adult life, served as a children's summer camp counselor for about fifteen years, and served as a vacation Bible school teacher for the past ten. He is currently teaching a senior adult Sunday school class and tells Bible stories to children fifth grade and under in evenings when needed.

He and his wife, Velma, have been married for sixty years and have a son, Scott, a daughter, Perian, two granddaughters, Megan Carson and Haley Metzner, and a grand-son-in-law, Paul Metzner.

Alph was written out of a strong desire to understand what it must have been like to have lived in Judah and Galilee during the time of Christ.

CAST OF CHARACTERS IN ALPHABETICAL ORDER

- Abe and Rebecca: Martha's parents
- Alph: son of Isaac: one of the two main characters
- Anna: Isaacs older sister and Simon's first wife: drowned in a storm
- Atticus: a Roman soldier
- Baby John: Simon and Mary's son
- Daniel: Mary's father, a metal smith: grandfather
- David and his wife Salome: Isaac's best friend and business partner
- Edfu: Isaac's friend on his return from Egypt: Uncle Edfu
- Eli and Elizabeth: Isaac's parents
- Eva: Isaac's wife: Alph's mother
- Isaac: Alph's father: eldest of the two main characters
- Isaac's four friends on his trip to Egypt
- James and John: sons of Zebedee: fishermen in Capernaum
- Jesus of Nazareth: the Messiah
- John: Simon and Mary's son
- John the Baptist
- Marie and Miriam: Alph and Martha's twin daughters

- Mary: Simon's wife: Daniel's daughter
- Mother Ruth: widowed neighbor who raised Isaac after his parents' death
- Nikos: Eva's father: Isaac's father-in-law: Grandpa: the potter
- Paul: the apostle
- Plato the donkey
- Rabbi Levy
- Ruth: Alph's younger sister: Timothy's wife
- Simon Peter and Andrew: brothers who are fishermen
- Simon: Isaac's brother-in-law: Alph's mentor: a carpenter
- Timothy: Ruth's husband: Alph's brother-in-law and best friend
- Zebedee: father of James and John: a fisherman

PROLOGUE TO THE
STORY OF ALPH

At about the time the Greco-Roman calendar turned from BC to AD there was a sprawling Roman city with mansions, paved streets and a thermal bath complex located on the western shore of the Sea of Galilee. Its name was Magdala and it had a population of about forty thousand people and a fleet of approximately two hundred thirty boats. Fish were plentiful on Galilee, and Magdala's large fish processing plant prepared dried and salted fish to be shipped to ports along the Mediterranean.

Capernaum was a much smaller village located on the northwestern shore of the Sea of Galilee, not far from where the Jordan River enters the sea. The area around Capernaum was very fertile and its location on the highway from the Mediterranean coast to Damascus made it a busy place. Merchants brought silk and spices from Damascus and took back the dried fish and fruits from the plains of Gennessaret. Despite its relative prosperity Capernaum was quite small. Its population was most likely no more than a thousand to fifteen hundred people. It was large enough however to host two small synagogues.

None of today's modern conveniences existed. There was no electricity, running water, phones, television, newspapers, books, or central heat and air. People walked, rode the back of an animal, or rode in a cart pulled by an animal. Goods were transported the same way. There was much, much more that we wouldn't have had living two thousand years ago; in Judah, in the early 100's A.D.

Even the geography of Israel was different at that time. The Jordan Rift Valley is part of the Great Rift Valley running from northern Syria to Mozambique in Africa. Much of it is below sea level. The Jordan River drains snow melt and rain from the higher elevations of the mountains in the north down to the Sea of Galilee, 702 feet below sea level, then on down to the Dead Sea, the lowest land on the face of the earth at 1388 feet below sea level. The Dead Sea doesn't drain. It evaporates. The Jordan runs in, the water evaporates, and over the centuries, its salinity has increased to 8.6 times that of the ocean. The people didn't know they were living below sea level in a crack between two of the earth's tectonic plates. It's a mountainous place that varies between arid and fertile land. The Jordan valley and its many small plains provided good farming, and sheep and goats did well among the hills.

Diets consisted of fish, mutton, fruits, vegetables, and olives. Grape vineyards produced grapes, juice, and wine. Wine was a staple at every meal. The Sea of Galilee provided an abundant supply of fish.

The only major city of size was Jerusalem, but the hills, plains, and shores of the Sea of Galilee and the western shore of the Mediterranean were covered with small towns and villages; even more than they are today. At the time of Christ, the land was occupied by Rome, whose main interest was collecting taxes. If the taxes were paid and the people were peaceful, Rome offered little or no interference with Jewish life. The people of Judah were united through their faith and the Law of Moses but divided geographically. Judah and the city of Jerusalem were located in the south of Israel and the land of Galilee was in the north. Between them lay the land of the Samaritans, a people whose ancestors had intermarried with the Canaanites. Their blood was mixed, and their children had lost the native language. They were despised by the Jews.

For the most part, education was sparse and left to the families. Middle-class boys received religious education and learned trades from the rabbi, their fathers, uncles, or other relatives. Girls received little formal education but learned the chores of the household from their mothers, grandmothers, and other older women in the family. When girls married they moved to the husband's family home. On the whole, life was peaceful, crime was low, and people took care of one another.

The story of *Alph* includes my impressions of Israel beginning between 01 and 10 A.D. about the time of the birth of Christ. This is life as I think it might have been. I used encyclopedias, history and geography books, and scripture as the historical basis for the story. I have done my best to understand Jewish life as it might have been then. The book begins during the childhood of Isaac, who becomes the patriarch of the story. Isaac is an affable, warm hearted ten-year-old, born and raised along the shores of the Sea of Galilee. The story continues to the time of Isaac's grandchildren. Isaac's son, Alph, follows in his father's footsteps, and their friends and family make my book. Isaac encounters some tough times in his young life, but come along with me and see how he handles them.

1

ISAAC THE YOUTH

In the coastal city of Magdala, on the Sea of Galilee, a fisher-man named Eli lived with his wife, Elizabeth, and their two children, twelve year old Anna, and four year old Isaac. Life was good and they were happy together. Elizabeth and Eli were friends throughout childhood but unfortunately, Elizabeth's parents didn't think Eli was a good catch for Elizabeth as a husband. In fact, they wouldn't even talk with his parents about arranging a marriage because they thought she could do better than marrying a fisherman. But, as time went by, it became obvious she was not going to find a prince to marry. Eventually they relented and gave the couple their blessing. Despite the reasonable life style the couple established, and the two beautiful children they produced, Elizabeth's parents still often made snide remarks about the inferiority of their son-in-law which caused grief in the family.

So, Eli and Elizabeth sold what they had and made the move from Magdala to Capernaum, a few miles up the coast on the north-western shore of Galilee. The fish market supplied the city and all the area of Capernaum with dried, pickled, and fresh fish. The Silk Road passed through Capernaum, and traders on the road purchased dried fish to be transported to Various Mediterranean seaports. In only a short time Eli launched a profitable fishing business for himself.

It didn't take long for the family to make friends and establish themselves in the community. Anna, who was eight years older than Isaac, grew into a lovely young woman and married a carpenter named Simon who had his own business. Isaac was also growing and was now a delightful and bright ten-year-old.

One morning young Isaac scarfed down his breakfast, then skipped out of the house and down the street. The house next door belonged to the widow Ruth, who was the first neighbor the family met when they moved to Capernaum. Ruth's husband had died several years before and she had no blood relatives. At fifty years old she became a grandmother figure to Anna and Isaac. She was roundish with her hair tied back and a perpetual smile on her face. Ruth must have invented cooking for she was forever dropping in with something baked or something stewed and it was always delicious. When Anna and Simon married, they moved into the house on the other side of Ruth, putting Ruth between Anna's house and Isaac's, making her a happy surrogate grandmother. But, this morning Isaac decided he should probably check and see how things were at Anna's.

She was busy grinding grain, and before Isaac could even get a word in she said, "Little brother of mine, why don't you go out to the wood shop and help Simon. I have to get this grain ground before I can cook another meal. Scoot along now, and we can talk later."

He knew enough to know that when she started with, "Little brother of mine," she meant business, and if he wanted to stay on friendly terms he should listen. So, he went out the back door to Simon's wood-shop. Isaac liked visiting Simon, because he was like a big brother and never fussed or scolded. He even let Isaac play in the shop while he worked. Ten is a good age to visit a wood-shop. He was fascinated by the carpenter tools and loved to watch Simon and play with the wood scraps, but Simon was particular about his tools. It was okay to use some of them if Simon wasn't working with them, but others he knew he was not to touch. Some were dangerous and others could easily get broken. Sometimes though, Simon would take time to show Isaac how to use and care for a tool, and then using it was okay. The special privilege made him feel like a professional carpenter. There was always plenty of sawdust for making roads and blocks of wood for make-believe donkeys and carts or mules pulling wagons; going to mysterious places with exotic loads.

Today, Simon was busy working on an order, so he went on down to the dock. The wooden surface of the dock was bleached white and worn smooth from daily scrubbing and the hundreds of times barefooted men had dragged their nets across it. Not one boat was at the dock when Isaac arrived. They were all out fishing, including his dad's. Three other crews worked from this dock next to the fish market. Isaac should have gotten there earlier to see everyone off to their catches for the day. It was important to him to talk to the fishermen and get them off to a good start. The fishermen all knew him well and talked to him like he was one of them, so that extra sleep he'd enjoyed this morning cost him an important highlight of the day.

Most of the children on his side of town were younger than him, not much fun for a ten-year-old. And, except for David, the teenagers didn't want a ten-year-old tagging along. David was sixteen. He was older than the other boys, but he was Isaac's friend.

One day, David said to Isaac, "Come on, we're going swimming. "Wow, swimming was something new to Isaac. His father had never taken him and although he had seen men swimming in the lake, no one had ever taught him. They walked up along the Jorden river from where it entered the Sea of Galilee until David found a place where the river was wide and a little over waste deep. He took off his clothes, stretched out his arms and fell forward, and with long easy strokes of his arms began gliding through the water. Isaac watched from the bank as David swam back and forth through the lazy river.

Finally, David stood up and called to Isaac. "Come down into the water with me. I'm going to teach you to swim."

So Isaac did. He took off his clothes and walked out into the water until it was pretty deep. David showed him what to do next. At first Isaac swallowed water and gaged as he tried to swim, but David held him up and kept working with him until he began to swim on his own. Isaac was soon swimming with no help. David told Isaac he thought he was part fish, but warned him to never go into deep water when he was alone. After that trip David and Isaac often went swimming when the weather was right.

But, this morning, David had a job mending nets and Isaac sat on one of the dock supporting posts with his chin in his hands looking up the street toward home. He thought to himself, "This is my side of town. I know everyone; the fishermen the residents that live here, the whole street and all the buildings. There's a house on the right where two old people live and then an empty lot and next to it is where Timothy, my other good friend lives. But, Timothy and his parents are gone to see his grandparents this week, so he isn't home to play with. Above Timothy's is an empty building that used to have some kind of business in it, but now it's empty. Across the street from it is my house and I'm back to where I started this morning." Then with a big sigh he thought, "The widow Ruth's, Anna and Simon's, a grove of trees, the dock and here I am, with nothing to do."

Then, Isaac decided to go exploring along the Jordan on his own. The water was flowing slow and easy and it was a beautiful, lazy day. He walked along the west bank, feeling the wet sand ooze between his toes. A few hundred yards up the river, a big rock jutted out over the water. Isaac took a seat on the sun warmed rock and stared into the cool clear water as it flowed past. A few small fish swam past, moving upstream in formation. He wondered where they were going. He climbed down from the rock and continued up the river until he came to a wide place where the water ran shallow over small rocks, making ripples in the stream. The rocks were worn smooth; their corners rounded by the water that had run over them for centuries. Slowly he began an inspection of the rocks until he found one that was just right for keeping. It was long, oval, and jet black with small streaks of color running through it. It just fit his hand and was too good not to keep.

Isaac heard a noise and looked up-river to see a lion lapping water on the same side he was inspecting. It was unusual for a lion to venture this far down from the mountains. Isaac was frozen in place as these things went through his mind and then he slowly and quietly turned, taking long, quiet strides, faster, and faster, until he was running as fast as he could go. Isaac was tall for a ten-year-old and those long skinny legs were moving in a blur. He could hear the lion right behind him. Its paws were making a padding sound and he could hear its panting breath. He didn't look back until he reached the front of the fish market, his chest heaving as he sucked in air to catch his breath. Suddenly he realized the noise of padding feet along the river's shore was him and the panting too, from running so hard. There was no sight of the lion and he no longer had his rock. He didn't know where he'd dropped it, but it didn't matter. He could get another rock, but he couldn't get another Isaac. Isaac thought Capernaum must be the best place in the world to live. There were so many places to go and things to do. He could visit nearby farms or go to the quarry and watch the men cut and size basalt blocks for building homes and businesses. He could watch people making oil with their olive presses or help Anna grind grain into flower. Soldiers often passed through from their barracks at the edge of town, traveling to other cities. Isaac liked to talk to them if they stopped for a break, and he loved to hear their stories.

One day Isaac's parents and his sister took his father's fishing boat to visit friends in Magdala. Isaac wanted to stay at home. Anna had a friend in Magdala, but Isaac had been only two when they moved to Capernaum and he would have no one to play with while his parents and Anna visited their friends. His mother gave him permission to stay at home and play in Simon's wood shop as long as he minded Simon and didn't bother him. She told him to go over to the widow Ruth's for lunch. Ruth liked Isaac and welcomed his company.

Isaac's father put the sail on his boat for the trip and it sped through the water much faster than rowing it. Anna lay down in the front of the boat and as she let her hand trail in the water wondered what young Isaac was doing. Normally he would stop by her house and visit every day when he made his rounds. Even though they were eight years apart they enjoyed each other's company.

In Magdala, Anna found her friend Esther, and they had a lot of business to catch up on. They needed to take a walk where they could talk without the "old" people around. Esther wanted to know all about Simon. How old was he? Was he handsome? Was he a good husband? How many children were they going to have? The list went on and on. Then Esther told Anna that she was going to be married. He also was a carpenter, and the girls just happened to be walking past where he was working. Esther said that if she was alone, the old busybodies would make something of her stopping to talk to her betrothed, but with Anna along it would be okay. When they reached where he was working, they slowed down until he could see them. She was glad Isaac was not along. He would go running up to inspect the work and give advice, embarrassing her. Anna had to admit he did seem to be a nice young man, but she didn't let on to Esther that her husband was a little better.

That evening, the family started home with all their friends standing on-shore to say goodbye. Eli used an oar to paddle his boat out to where he could set sail. The wind was going to be against them, and he was going to have to tack in order to sail into it. He hoisted the sail, and just as he went to swing the boom, his foot slipped and at the same time the wind caught the sail and swung the boom way out, with Eli hanging on. His weight tipped the boat until it started to take on water. Anna and Elizabeth both screamed and Eli went into the water to try to save the boat. It was too late. It all happened so fast, and Eli could do nothing. People on shore saw the boat sinking but had no way to help. All three went under the water with the boat. Eli's last thoughts were of his son. Who would teach Isaac and bring him up in the proper way for a Jewish boy. Elizabeth too, took her last breath thinking of her son. Who would care for Isaac's clothes and see that he was fed, and Anna also, was crying out, who will love and care for my precious little brother? In a matter of a couple of minutes Isaac became an orphan.

Back in Capernaum was a young carpenter, widowed almost as soon as he had become a husband and a ten-year-old boy with no family. A runner was sent with the terrible news, but who should it be to tell them? It was decided it should be Rabbi Levy.

As Rabbi Levy began telling the story Isaac's mind raced ahead of him and he figured it out long before the Rabbi got that far. His eyes welled with tears and he began to moan. He started running; running as fast as when he thought the lion was chasing him. He ran up his street, out of town and out into the middle of a grain field where he fell on the ground, crying and moaning until there was no energy left in him. He stayed away from the city, and no one knew where he was.

A few days later, a man came to Ruth's house looking for Isaac. He said he was Isaac's grandfather and had come to take the boy home. He said he had a room for Isaac and would provide for his needs. In return, Isaac would work in his shop, sweeping floors and making deliveries. He would have every Sabbath off, and on that day he could rest. Ruth said she didn't know where Isaac was, but she would try to find him. Isaac's mother, and Ruth had been good friends and she had told Ruth on several occasions of the problems they had with her parents.

Later in the day, Ruth saw Isaac at his house, so she went over and told him about his grandfather, of what he said, and that he wanted to take him home. Isaac's eyes got big and reflected fear.

"I know all about my grandfather," Isaac said. "And I don't want to go with him." With that, he ran away.

When Isaac's grandfather returned, Ruth wasn't sure what to say, and the first thing that came to mind was just to tell him that Isaac was not there. The man became furious. With his outburst and with what Elizabeth had told her about him, and from Isaac's fear, she knew that Isaac had no business leaving with this man.

She knew it was at least partly a lie, but she said to him, Isaac has friends all over town, and I have no idea where he might be or when I will see him again. I couldn't tell you where to look.

With that, the man's face turned beet red, and he shouted, "I don't have time for foolishness like this. He will probably be as lazy as his father anyway." And he stormed off up the road the way he had come.

That was the last anyone ever saw of him.

Isaac's father had been a fisherman, and the only inheritance Isaac could claim was a small, three-room house. Evan the boat was gone. Isaac was alone. Simon was his brother-in-law, but he wasn't a blood relative. Simon and Isaac each grieved in his own way, not knowing what to say or how to console the other. Friends and neighbors offered to take Isaac in to raise, but he refused help, often sleeping on the streets of Capernaum rather than going home to the empty house.

Ruth refused to leave a ten-year-old boy to fend for himself. Her husband had died before they'd had children, and like Isaac, she had no blood family. Isaac had never known what to call this cheerful, middle-aged widow. She was too old for him to call her Ruth. The neighborhood kids called her Mother Ruth, but that hadn't sounded right to Isaac. He'd always just referred to her as their neighbor. Now he decided to call her Mother Ruth too.

Isaac was offered a job to help with a thorough cleaning of the fish market. He enjoyed working, and the money they paid him, meager though it was would help Mother Ruth with her household expenses. His job was to carry water up from the lake to wash everything down.

At the end of one hard day, Isaac was bone tired. He collected his pay and headed toward home.

The front of the fish market was L shaped, and there was some tall grass at the inside corner of the building where no one ever walked. The grass had died from its summer growth and had fallen over. To tired Isaac, it looked like an inviting place to make a bed for the night. He pulled some of the grass, piled it in the corner, and curled up on it. It was soft, and he was warm and comfortable lying in the corner shielded from the wind. Unknown to him, though, the north wind was coming down off of Mount Hermon. As the temperature dropped, a rare snow-fall started, and by the time the cold air woke him, his teeth were chattering. Bare footed Isaac started running through the snow for Mother Ruth's house.

When he arrived, Mother Ruth was awake, worried about where the boy might be. When she saw how cold he was, she took him to her bed, laid him down, and curled up behind him. Isaac was cold. Right now he missed his mother, and as the warmth from the blanket and Ruth's body began to take away his chill, he began to cry. Before long he began to relax and went to sleep.

When Isaac awoke, Mother Ruth had a fire going and was cooking breakfast. It took a few minutes for him to relax and remember what had happened and where he was. Mother Ruth told him that while she finished baking him some cakes, he was to go home and bring his bedding and clothes over to her house. She had a small room he could have, and he was going to live with her. Isaac offered no resistance, and from then on they were family. His house became a kind of storage building for them. Isaac found firewood, helped around the house and did odd jobs for the market. The few coins he made he either saved or gave to Mother Ruth to help with the house. Sometimes Simon would come by to visit and have dinner, and after a while they reached the point where they could laugh and tell stories together as they had done in older times.

Isaac still longed for his old life. He missed his parents and sister, but the grief of his loss got easier to take as time passed.

Ruth decided she needed to talk to the rabbi. She knew nothing of Isaac's education; what he knew about God, whether or not he could read and write, whether he could do numbers, or was skilled at anything of use. Of course at ten years old, he wouldn't have learned much, but she didn't know if he knew anything. So one day as soon as Isaac had left the house, she went to see Rabbi Levy. "I am concerned about the boy. I know nothing of his education and am afraid he may be way behind."

"I agree that Isaac may be way behind," Rabbi Levy said. "I know nothing of his studies, or where he is with his education. Isaac's father used to bring him to synagogue on the Sabbath but beyond that, I have no knowledge of the boy's education. My recommendation is to start him in school right away. I will discover what Isaac knows, and then go from there. Ruth, you are doing a great job as mother, but the boy needs a father's influence. I will talk to Simon. Between the two of us we will do our best to be fathers to him, or at least father and big brother. Tell Isaac, 'Go see Rabbi Levy right away.' I will work with the boy."

The next morning, Isaac appeared at the school next door to the synagogue. Rabbi Levy didn't know what to expect. Would Isaac rebel at attending school; and skip attendance, or would he have to be talked to and encouraged for it to be in his best interest? The rabbi was surprised.

"Papa talked to me a lot about God," Isaac said. "And when we were out together we used to play games speaking other languages. He taught me to speak Greek, Hebrew and of course I already knew Aramaic, and he had just started teaching me to read and write it."

The rabbi also discovered that he had some knowledge of numbers. He thought to himself, "What a remarkable young man this is. I would never have dreamed there was that much knowledge in that little head."

"I haven't been trying to keep it a secret," Isaac said. "It just never came up."

Rabbi Levy said, "Isaac, in not more than three years it will be time for your bar mitzvah. You will have a lot of work to do to get ready for it."

Isaac was excited. He was going to school and bar mitzvah.

He liked to study the book of Proverbs. He remembered that Papa used to have a proverb for everything. He had told Isaac there were two proverbs he should always remember. One was, "Don't neglect your mother's teachings, for they are a graceful wreath on your head; and beads for your neck." The other one was, "Don't let sinners entice you; don't go on the path with them; keep your feet from their way, because their feet run to evil." Papa also said not to reject the instruction of the Lord, or to despise his correction, because the Lord loves those he corrects, just like a father who treats his son with favor. Papa had a proverb for every occasion. Isaac hoped that when he got older, he would be like his papa. As young as Isaac was he thought his papa was probably a pretty good man. Rabbi Levy said he was.

Isaac helped provide for Mother Ruth and himself by doing odd jobs, while Ruth taught him to cook, and Rabbi Levy taught him to read, wright, and do numbers. He went to Synagogue every Sabbath too. Isaac was growing up to be a good boy as well as a handsome one. He was starting to fill out from that skinny kid that was all arms and legs, with a little more meat and muscle on his bones, and his smiling and pleasant countenance was known to almost everyone in Capernaum.

Isaac had made a good choice in friends with David. David was older and hopefully wiser. One day when Isaac was almost thirteen, he and David went swimming. David had noticed that Isaac was starting to get a shadow of a mustache and a few chin whiskers, and when they stripped down to swim, he saw that Isaac was starting to get some body hair. He asked him what Simon or the rabbi had told him about girls.

"Nothing," Isaac said. "Girls are just girls, and then they grow up and become mothers."

David was still single, but he was eighteen years old with considerably more experience in life than Isaac. From asking a few more questions, David was able to tell that neither Simon nor the rabbi had spoken a word to Isaac about the birds and bees. David decided that both Simon and the rabbi didn't want to tackle the issue and were hoping the other would have the talk with Isaac or that it would just miraculously go away. He guessed he would have to be the miracle.

David waited for the chance he was looking for, and it soon came. Three girls that were from farther in the city were walking toward the river. He wasn't sure that what he was doing was right, but he knew the girls and knew that their character wasn't of the most innocent type. This didn't ease his conscience any, but he went on with his plan. Isaac was hanging around the fish market but wasn't working. David went by and asked him to go for a walk with him. Once they left the fish market, he told Isaac to follow him, to be quiet, and not ask him any questions until he said he could.

"Why?" Isaac said.

"I told you to be quiet," David said, "And you have started already. Now don't say another word – and I mean not another word! – Until we get back here. Just nod your head yes if you understand."

Isaac nodded his head, and they walked on. Just before they got to the swimming hole, they heard the girls laughing and splashing. David stopped and put his finger to his lips for quiet and gave Isaac a hard look. There was grass growing on the hill before the swimming hole, and David got down on all fours and motioned Isaac to do the same. They crept quietly through the grass until they could see the river. They could see the naked girls having a big time in the water.

David let Isaac look for several minutes and then tapped him on the shoulder and motioned for them to back out. When they got back down the path, David looked at Isaac. His face was red and his eyes were large and when they reached the fish market, David said, "Let's go over to the log by the lake and talk for a while."

After they sat down David said, "Well, Isaac, do you have any questions?"

He did. Lots of questions, and they talked for much of the rest of the afternoon. After a while the girls walked by and waved. David smiled at them and waved back, but Isaac stared up into the sky like he didn't notice them. David still didn't know if he had been wrong to give this part of Isaac's education to him, especially the way he started it, but it worked and brought on all the questions he needed to answer to satisfy Isaac's curiosity. After that day, Isaac occasionally asked a question of David, but neither Simon nor the rabbi ever said a word to him about male and female differences and relationships. David did make sure that Isaac understood that girls were to be respected, and when the day came that he met a girl and fell in love with her, he was to treat her with tenderness and respect.

He also told Isaac that their trip to the swimming hole was the only one he ever needed to make. "It isn't right to spy on girls just for a thrill," he said, "and I'm not sure we should have done it as part of your adult education, but I didn't know any other way."

On the last Sabbath before he reached his thirteenth year Isaac made his Bar Mitzvah. This signified he had become a full-fledged member of the Jewish community and now had the responsibilities that come with that status. These included moral responsibilities for his own actions, eligibility to read from the Torah, and the right to lead or participate in a minyan. He could also possess personal property, be legally married according to Jewish law, and he had to follow the six hundred and thirteen laws of the Torah. Mother Ruth prepared a party for him, and they celebrated his becoming a man.

When he reached sixteen, Isaac decided there was nothing to keep him in the hill country of Galilee. He decided to try life in Jerusalem. And so began his journey.

2

LEAVING HOME TO EXPLORE THE WORLD

If there was anything lacking in Isaac, it was his experience in picking friends. In Capernaum he knew everyone. Everyone was kind to him and he was used to the gentle-folk of his home-town. After six months in Jerusalem, he had made strong friendships of four homeless young men of not really bad, but questionable character. One evening when they were trying to decide on an interesting adventure, one of them suggested a long journey to Egypt. Isaac was fluent in both Hebrew and Aramaic and figured he could pick up some Egyptian on the trip. This would get him by, and they could get jobs with some traders traveling in a caravan. At sixteen Isaac was tall and had a full black beard, was well muscled, and had a pleasant countenance. People thought he was older than he really was, and unless he was asked he let them think what they would. So, Isaac's journey continued.

The boys found jobs working as camel drivers in a caravan. The owner taught them to load camels, feed, water, and even bathe them. Each boy was assigned a camel, and when the trip began, it was their job to take care of their animal. They were to lead it, following the camel ahead of them. Admittedly, there was nothing to the job. Isaac's camel followed the one ahead of it with no prompting. In fact, when they stopped for trading, food, rest, and water, he had no concern in getting his camel back in line. It knew on start-up which camel to follow. Their weather was hot and dusty, and their travel was all walking, but Isaac soon began to like his job.

Their journey followed a zigzag route, stopping in places to unload some things and reload others. It took five months to reach Egypt. When they arrived in Goshen, they unloaded their camels, received their pay, and were told the caravan was being disbanded until the next season.

It didn't take long for five boys to find enough excitement to spend their money. Isaac however was thriftier than the others and used to saving his money, so he tied it in a cloth in his pack to keep for the future. One day after the boys' money was gone, hunger began to set in, and as they were walking through the marketplace, two of the boys stole jewelry from a merchant, thinking they could sell it for food. They ran through the shops and crowds, leaving a trail of upset carts and scattered merchandise. The merchant ran behind them yelling "Thieves, thieves, someone stop those thieves." The boys had almost gotten away when they ran straight into the arms of three Egyptian soldiers. After questioning the out-of-breath merchant, the soldiers returned his stolen property, tied the two boys together and led them off.

After a couple of days, Isaac and the other two boys attempted to see the thieves, but were told by soldiers at the jail that the boys were being well cared for, and they had best go on. The next morning, Isaac awoke to find his two remaining friends gone. None of their belongings remained, but at least they hadn't gone through his and found his money stash. He remembered one of his father's proverbs, "Don't let sinners entice you; don't go on the path with them; keep your feet from their way, because their feet run to evil."

After a couple of days wandering through Goshen by himself, Isaac came across a caravan ready to leave for Damascus. They were looking for another camel driver and after Isaac elaborated on his experience (and embellished it just a little) the man in charge of the caravan gave him the job. The next day they left, following the same route Isaac had followed on his trip down.

The trip went well for three months, as they stopped to unload and reload in some small town or settlement after another. Then, when they were well into the wilderness one of the other camel drivers became violently ill. The caravan stopped for a whole day for the poor man, but when he wasn't getting any better, the caravan leader announced that they had to go on. They couldn't afford the food and water it would take for the whole caravan to be stopped while he got well enough to travel. It was obvious that if they left him there he would die, but there was no other choice. They had to leave him or put the whole caravan in jeopardy.

Isaac volunteered to stay there with the man. Everyone thought it was foolhardy on Isaac's part, because they were sure the man would die anyway and Isaac would be left alone in the wilderness to suffer who knows what on his own, bur Isaac insisted. The merchant who owned the caravan was a good man and said the best he could do was to give them half of their pay, a goatskin of water, and a ration of food for each of them. Some of the men helped Isaac get him under the shade of a bush, and the caravan went on.

The man's skin was black, but tinged with red from the fever, and wet with sweat. Isaac tried to feed him a little and give him a few sips of water several times a day, but he wasn't improving any. If anything, his fever was getting higher. A few more days passed and they were almost out of food and water. Now what would they do?

Isaac started walking in a circle around the camp searching for a water source. Each round moved him our farther and farther. After several hours he was almost out of the site of their camp. He found a long stick, tied a piece of clothing to it and stuck it in the ground by their camp. This allowed him to travel out much farther and still keep site of camp. Finally he came to a rocky low area with a lot of green vegetation in the bottom of the lowest part. He found a thin flat rock, and taking it like a hoe, he began to dig. After a while the sand began to get damp, and a while longer, his hole began to fill with water. He had found a spring, out here in the middle of nowhere. He tasted the water and it was sweet. He ran back to camp and got their goat skin, and filled it with water. One problem was solved. Now what would they do for food?

Again, Isaac began his circling. He didn't know what he was looking for. Which plants in this arid area were edible and which could be poisonous? He started by feeling for tender leaves, then touching them to his tongue, and finally eating a small amount. He pulled up a few small plants and tasted the roots. Some of his plant tests were bitter, some puckered his lips, and others just tasted bad. Finally he chose the leaves and roots of three different plants that all tasted pretty good. He filled his hat with roots and leaves, washed them at his spring, and then prepared their first wilderness meal. He gave his new friend water but withheld the food until he had tested it. The next morning he was feeling fine so he went ahead and fed his patient some crushed leaves.

Several more days passed and the man's temperature began to drop. So far his speech had made no sense to Isaac but now he could tell some words. The man must be speaking some Egyptian dialect. Whatever it was, it was a language unfamiliar to Isaac. He tried his languages and found that the man could speak Aramaic. This became their language for communication.

"What is your name?" Isaac asked.

"Edfu," the man said. It is an Egyptian name, and your name would be Alph."

"No." Isaac said. "My name is Isaac."

"That is the name given you by your parents, but in my language you are Alph."

"No. My name is Isaac."

"Yes, that is the name given you by your parents but in my language you are Alph."

"Why is it Alph?" Isaac said.

"In my dialect Alph is the name given to kind, caring, and compassionate people." Edfu said. "That is what I will call you, Alph" Because you have saved my life."

"I am from a small town in Galilee," Isaac Said. "It is called Capernaum. Where are you from?"

"I am from a small village way up the Nile," Edfu replied. "It is many days walk from Goshen where our caravan started. I have been working on camel caravans for over twenty years."

As the two men talked and became friends, they shared stories of their homes, the dreams they had, and what would someday be. They became colleagues, good friends, and equals, although Edfu was old enough to be Isaac's father.

It was time to get Edfu on his feet. Isaac bent over, pulled one of Edfu's arms up over his shoulders, and then straightened up. Slowly Edfu straightened out his legs and came to his full height. Isaac was surprised. When the caravan was moving he had seen Edfu at a distance and noticed he was very tall, but when he got to his feet he was more than a head taller than Isaac, and Isaac wasn't short. "Are all of your people as tall as you?" said Isaac.

"People of my tribe are all tall," Edfu said. "But I am the shortest in my family. I have two sisters who are taller than I."

Edfu had no fat on him. His bones, especially his elbows and knees, were big and knobby. If his body were padded with flesh he would be a huge man, but as he is, he is very tall and lanky.

After a few days of walking around the camp, Edfu decided he was strong enough to walk. He was ready to start again. So, they filled their goatskin with water and their sacks with leafs and roots, and began the rest of their journey together.

The first few days were slow, but Edfu began to pick up his pace and his stamina surprised Isaac. A few days went by, then a week and as the days passed they walked and talked and their friendship grew. Edfu insisted on referring to Isaac as Alf.

Thus far they had seen no wild animals or game of any kind. This didn't stop Edfu from worrying about it. The caravans he had worked for years had the security of numbers, but here were two lone men walking across an arid wilderness with no weapon to protect themselves. They were left to chance and good luck.

One day Edfu said to Alf, "I wish I knew the names of the gods that live in this area, so we could pray to them and offer a sacrifice for our safety."

"Edfu," Isaac said, "There is only one true God, the Lord of Israel. He is the only true God, the God that created heaven and earth, all plant life, all animals, the birds, and the fish. Then he created man in his image to rule over the earth that he had created, but there was a problem. Man would not obey God. All that God had asked man to do was to love him with all his might, soul, and strength, and his neighbor as himself. But, man couldn't do that. He proved too selfish, sometimes unloving, and unfaithful to God. So God punished him by letting outside warriors conquer the men he had created and then after a while he would let them start over again, but the result was always the same. God is a good and loving God. If we are the same way, he will take care of us.

Edfu had never before heard of these things and asked Isaac to tell him more of this God he was talking about. So, they walked for days with Isaac telling Edfu of the many things he learned in school. Edfu was pleased to hear them and wanted to hear more. Isaac talked and talked, telling Edfu all the history of God and man until he had no more stories, and Edfu could think of no more questions.

Then Isaac suggested that as they walked, they could pass the time by teaching each other a new language. Isaac wanted to learn to speak Egyptian, and Edfu wanted to learn Hebrew. Their language classes went on for hours and the days passed quickly.

Another week passed and they had not seen a well or spring for a long time. Their water which they had so carefully rationed was almost gone. The day finally came when their goatskin was down to just mouthfuls. Isaac insisted that Edfu drink the last of the water. They found a little shade during the day, and as evening began to cool they started walking. By morning they were exhausted. The sun was coming up, and before long the heat would again drain what little energy they had left. Edfu dragged his feet as he walked and Isaac staggered along. They knew if they stopped they would be done.

And then Isaac saw a wisp of smoke ahead. It had to be someone cooking. Their pace picked up and if they could have, they would have run. They could see a few houses ahead and the trees of an oasis. As they got closer they saw two children coming toward them, each carrying a jug of water. Isaac and Edfu said nothing as they collapsed on the ground and gulped down the cool, wet, sweet, wonderful, water.

There were two families at the oasis. They took care of the spring for caravans passing through and were paid and given food for their work in keeping the water clean and flowing. The boy and girl were brother and sister and the only children in the two families. It was a lonely existence, but the only life they knew. Twice each year, the families alternated making a trip into Jerusalem with a caravan.

Isaac loved telling stories so he entertained the children for a few days while he and Edfu rested. The boy taught Isaac how to travel in the shade with a camel. You can't travel directly into or away from the sun, but if you tacked to the left for a while and then to the right for the same length of time, you could walk beside the camel in its shade.

After a few days of rest Isaac gave the families some money for the food they had eaten and some to take with them; they packed their sacks, filled their goatskin, and were again on their way. The families told Isaac and Edfu that they could be in Jerusalem within three to four days of steady walking.

After the second day, they began to see an occasional village and even some shepherds with their flocks. They were going to make it. The Lord had provided, they were alive and well. On the fourth morning, they came to the top of a small hill and there it was. They could see the walls of the holy city. Jerusalem itself was straight ahead.

That evening, they sat in the market-place and talked of their journey. Edfu dreamed of home but more of joining another caravan and traveling as he had done for so many years. Dust, sand, and camels were in his blood. It was his way of life.

Isaac had become homesick and had had enough adventure. He decided to head home to Galilee to fish, while Edfu looked for another caravan going back to Egypt. Their journey was over. It was time for each to go his way. Isaac had become quite fond of Edfu. The companionship they had shared in their wilderness journey had formed a brotherly bond between them. Edfu's near-death experience, Isaac's determination to overcome adversity, and the dry, hot days, and cold nights they'd shared had made them more than just friends. They were family, about to separate, never to see one another again. Isaac had become a man; Edfu had gained a dear brother, his little brother, Alph, a family member he had never before enjoyed. The two were changed forever.

That night they slept on the ground under some trees, as they had often done in the past few months. In the morning they embraced and bid one another good-bye. "Take care of my young friend Alph," Edfu said, and watched as Isaac disappeared down the road to Jericho. Then he turned and started walking toward a caravan being made up just outside of the city.

3

NIKOS DECIDES TO MOVE

A sixteen-year-old girl named Eva was raised in the Roman city of Antioch, a city on the convergence of three land routes and one sea route. Trade was passed from caravan to caravan, from ship to caravan, and from caravan to ship as trading goods were moved throughout the Roman Empire. In fact, Antioch was considered the capital of the Eastern Empire. It was also a vacation city, with many visitors and transients moving about.

Eva's father, a Greek named Nikos, had a profitable pottery business. His decorative pottery was some of the best and much desired by traders. He and Eva lived in the pottery shop, and with only the two of them to support, Nikos had been able to save a sizable amount of his income.

His problem was not his income but his daughter, Eva. Nikos was a short, stocky, muscular man with wavy black hair and beard; nice but not a good looking man. Eva on the other hand had her father's black wavy hair but that was where her inherited looks ended. Her complexion was as clear, soft, and creamy as a baby's. Her eyes were dark, deep set, tender, and crinkled around the edges when she smiled, which was much of the time. The looks she received from boys made Nikos' heart stop and the older she got the more he wanted to find a better place for them to live. She was just reaching marrying age and Nikos saw no signs of a prospective son-in-law in Antioch.

Nikos decided that they should leave Greece. They needed a change, a new start; in a new place. A friend of Nikos had often talked of a village he had visited in Galilee, located on the northern shore of the Sea of Galilee. He said the people there were kind, honest, and friendly. There was not the constant push in business to make more money or a name for yourself. It sounded like just the place he would like to take his daughter. The town was Capernaum. It was the main city of the area and had every kind of small business imaginable and welcomed all people. Nikos' friend told him he had seen no pottery shops or manufacturers of pottery in the area and should be ripe for business. Nikos dreamed of introducing his pottery to such a community.

Word got around that Nikos' shop was for sale, and it wasn't long until people were looking at it. Several who looked would have liked to buy it but didn't have the money. One man had been there several times and really wanted the place but just couldn't raise the money for the purchase. One morning, he stopped in front of Nikos' shop leading a little donkey pulling a cart.

He approached Nikos with a smile on his face, "Nikos! How are you today? I have been wondering how you are going to move to Capernaum after you have sold your property?"

"I suppose," Nikos said, "I will have to purchase a pack animal that we can load our belongings on to make the trip."

"Think of this," His friend said. "I have in front of your establishment a little brown, one-year-old donkey, not quite fully grown. He comes complete with harness and nearly a new donkey cart. I offer you all the money I have and my donkey and cart for your business.

It was not what Nikos had imagined, but it sounded like what he needed. He thought about it for a minute but the man was watching him and he couldn't think. Nikos turned his back to him and walked toward the back of the shop, his head was down, and he was pulling on his beard in contemplation. The value of the donkey wasn't much compared to the difference in his price and what the man had in cash. No one who had looked at the shop had said he was asking too much. He knew the value, but this man was trying. He wanted it badly to start a business but just didn't have the money. If Nikos hung on till the right person came along it could sell for far more than he was asking. Did he want to help the man live his dream with his business? Did he want to take what he could get now and get out? He had enough savings to give it away and relocate in Capernaum with money to spare if he wanted.

This is a nice man. I am going to help him, get my daughter out of here, and start over. He let go of his beard, raised his head, and walked back to the front of the shop with a smile on his face. "I suppose you know that the price you can afford to give me for this building is far less than it is worth, but I have measured it in my head. You are a good man; I want to take my daughter, our belongings and leave. Please take the building for what you have offered me and I hope your new business prospers."

Nikos went outside and looked at the donkey. There was a short rope on the donkey's bridal. He took a hold of it and attempted to lead the donkey. I wouldn't move. He spoke to it and slapped it on the rump, but it still didn't, move. He went back inside and said, "Your donkey isn't well trained. Either that or it is extremely stubborn.

"The donkey is young and not yet trained, but I assure you he is in good health, can pull a hefty load, and work all day. His name is 'Donkey.' If you call him by name he will respond."

While the men were talking, Eva went outside, spoke in the donkey's ear, and started walking away. The donkey followed her. She turned around and walked back and again the donkey followed her. She talked to him some more and came inside. The donkey turned his head and watcher her enter the building.

"Papa," she said. "What is the donkey's name?"

"This man said he calls him 'donkey.'"

"That's no name for a donkey. I'm going to call him Plato. He's smart and understands me when I talk to him."

"What did you say to him," said Nikos.

"I just told him how cute and smart he was, and if he were my donkey I would take very good care of him."

Nikos just shook his head, understanding that the donkey was going to be a pet for Eva as much as a beast of burden for them to use in moving.

The two men agreed that Nikos would be out in not more than two weeks and the man should give him the money before that time.

The men parted and Eva found a long rope and tied Plato to the back of the building. She put some grain in a bowl, got a large pot, filled it with water, pulled some green grass, and piled it up for him, and then scratched him behind his ears. For the next two weeks Eva went outside and talked to Plato every chance she had, and made sure he always had fresh grass and water.

Eva and Nikos spent the next week sorting, packing, and getting ready to move. Nikos built a box on the front of the cart for their food and personal supplies. He put his work tools, clothing, bedding and supplies in the rest of cart. When the packing was finished and the cart was loaded Nikos began to worry if Plato could pull the cart. He estimated that the cart might be as much as twice Plato's weight. The wheels of the cart carried almost all of the cart's weight, but all of the hills they would be traversing would be a hard pull for Plato. Niko told Eva that when they came to a hill they would push on the back of the cart to help Plato and going downhill they could drag their feet to keep it from pushing on him too hard.

Eva agreed and the next morning they said good-bye to friends and began their journey to Capernaum in Galilee.

The day went well but it was long, and when they stopped for the night all three of them were tired. Eva put some blankets on the ground, and Nikos unhitched Plato from the cart and started gathering firewood. Eva pulled some grass from along the road and piled it up for Plato, along with a little grain for him. She put out a bowl and poured him some water from their goatskin. Then she started their meal.

It was dark when they finished eating, and Nikos gathered some more firewood for the night. With the sun going down it would get cold, so Eva curled up on one side of the blanket. Plato stood watching her for a while and then lay on the ground next to her. By the middle of the night the temperature had dropped sharply and the heat from Plato's body made a cozy place for Eva to sleep.

The first rays of the sun woke them, and after eating, Nikos hitched Plato to the cart and told Eva they were going to travel differently. They would stop and rest a few minutes when they crossed a stream and fill their goatskin with water. During the heat of the day they would stop and rest for a couple of hours and let Plato graze. This way they could conserve their energy. Ten days to two week of days like yesterday would leave them exhausted before they ever reached Capernaum.

On the fifth night, they hadn't much more than gotten to sleep when Plato got to his feet and started braying. This was the first time they had heard him bray and they had no idea he could be so loud. Plato went into the brush beside the camp and furious noises ensued with hissing, braying, and the breaking of brush. In just a few minutes everything became quiet. Plato's hoofs hit the ground a couple of more times and then it got quiet again.

A moment later he returned to camp and lay down. Eva spoke to him but he just laid still. She could hear his even breathing as he went back to sleep. At first light Nikos carefully looked through the brush. There was a large, very dead cat that had been generously stomped to death. He inspected Plato, but other than some claw marks on his legs, he was in good shape. Plato now had one more attribute. He was a beast of burden, pet, and now defender of his family.

LEE CARSON

Some of the hills were pretty steep and long. Sometimes they had to stop and rest before they continued, but a little at a time, they made their way. About the nineteenth day they asked some traders they passed how far it was to Capernaum. They were told it was an easy two day travel, mostly downhill. This bolstered their spirits and they stopped for some lunch.

Nikos was out in the woods along the road gathering firewood, and Plato was grazing alongside the road the other direction when two rough-looking men walked up behind Eva. When she turned around and saw them, one of them said, "Are you traveling alone girlie?"

Before anyone could move, Eva screamed and Plato came charging in at top speed. He grabbed one man's arm, giving him a good bite, while the other started running. As soon as the bitten man could get loose, he ran after the other, with Plato braying and running after him. Then Plato turned and came back to Eva, nuzzling her neck and making a little gurgling sound. By this time Nikos was back and they both marveled that this trip could ever have happened without their friend and guardian with them.

Another day and a half and they were coming into Capernaum. As they came into town they saw Mother Ruth and stopped for information.

4

CAPERNAUM GAINS NEW RESIDENTS

Isaac went to the fish market early one morning looking for day work. Located between the market and the Sea of Galilee was a large fishpond. Fishermen could bring their boats into a little man-made fishing port, about waist deep, next to the pond. From there they could stand in the water next to their boats and move fish from their nets to the pond with buckets. A "fish counter" kept track of the fish as they were transferred from net to pond, and one member of the fishing crew would count with him. If they messed up on the count, either the market owner or the fishermen would be on their necks. It was an important job. The market poured several buckets of water over into the pond every day and fed the fish to keep a fresh supply for their customers. People traveled from all over Galilee just to get fresh fish. Today the market wasn't accepting any fish until evening. The fishermen had been notified ahead of time that they were draining the pond and cleaning it, so it would be healthy for the fish. The market owner told Isaac he could use him all day.

By evening Isaac was really tired. They had drained the pond, scrubbed the rocks that lined it, and filled it with fresh water. The sun was getting low in the sky as he trudged home.

As he neared home, he saw a donkey cart stopped outside Mother Ruth's house. She was speaking in Greek to a man and a girl. Isaac didn't even know Mother Ruth could speak Greek. When they stopped speaking, Mother Ruth introduced them as Nikos and his daughter, Eva. Isaac immediately became tongue tied. Eva was the most beautiful girl he had ever seen. She had fair skin, beautiful long, black, curly hair, and gorgeous deep black eyes. He wanted to stare, but was afraid to look at her.

Mother Ruth broke the silence by explaining that Nikos was a potter and had come to town because he heard there was no potter for miles around. He thought it would be an ideal place to set up a pottery shop. Nikos explained that he made all kinds of bowls, pots, and plates for cooking, storage, and serving food as well as decorative pots and vases. All he needed was an ample supply of clay for his work.

For right now all they needed was a place to stay. Mother Ruth thought that maybe Nikos could stay with Isaac for a while and Eva could stay with her. Isaac didn't think he had ever heard a more wonderful plan, but about all he could do was grunt that it would be okay. So the deal was struck. He and Mother Ruth would supply food and lodging for their guests, who might possibly decide to become new citizens of Capernaum. Most of the citizens of Capernaum were Jews, and a Greek family might very well be a welcome mix to the main city of Galilee.

The next morning after breakfast, Isaac took Nikos on a tour of Capernaum. After they returned home, Nikos told Isaac he would be alright by himself to wander around looking at this and that and spending some time alone to think out what he must do. After a couple of days, Nikos decided on an empty building with one large front room that could be used for a shop and two smaller rooms in back for him and Eva. It was just across the street from Isaac's and Mother Ruth's homes. Nikos decided to rent the building for his shop and home, and then, of course Isaac was right there, seeing if he could assist Capernaum's newest residents.

Nikos walked the hills behind his shop and found a large deposit of clay only a short way from his shop, more than he would ever need. Isaac and Eva started clearing the land over the vein of clay. They cleared all the vegetation, rocks, brush, and top soil covering the clay. Now it would just be a matter of digging the clay and getting it to the shop. It wasn't far down to the sea shore, and the water Nikos would need could easily be carried in buckets.

Nikos had brought all of his hand tools with him in the donkey cart, but there were two tools he would have to build. He needed a pottery wheel and a furnace to bake his products. The pottery wheel was constructed from wood, and Isaac got Simon to look at Nikos' sketches. Simon said it wouldn't be hard to build. He would have to build a frame, on which he would mount a vertical rotating shaft. There would be two wheels, one on the top and one on the bottom of the shaft. The potter would sit down with his feet on the lower wheel, and the clay would be placed on the upper wheel. When the potter rotated the wheel assembly with his feet, the clay would rotate, and the potter would mold the clay with his hands as it spun. They dug a place for the furnace into the hill beside the shop and carried wood from the forest on the hills behind the shop to fire it.

Nikos and Eva took wooden buckets up the hill to their clay pit, filled them with clay, and drug them down the hill. Simon built the pottery wheel, and Nikos was soon making pots; big pots, small pots, bowls, platters and all sorts of household utensils. Business was good and Nikos soon began making hand molded sculptures. Isaac thought Nikos' sculptures were the most beautiful he had ever seen, although he hadn't seen much.

Nikos' business was so good he was having a hard time keeping up production to cover his sales. He decided to offer Isaac a regular full time job. Now Isaac had an excuse to be near Eva every day. The first thing he did was to build a sled on which he could scoot loads of clay down the hill from the clay pit. Since it was downhill, he could easily load four buckets of clay on the sled, and drag them down the hill to the shop.

One day, Nikos ran out of clay, and Isaac took his sled and buckets up the hill. He soon had a full load of clay and started down the hill. There was a small swag in the road and Isaac got up enough speed to get across it. About half way across he stumbled and fell, but the sled kept coming and slid over Isaac's leg. He knew instantly he was in trouble. His leg really hurt and was sticking out at a peculiar angle. It was broken for sure, but he couldn't move, and he was too far from the shop for anyone to hear him.

The sun was beginning to get low in the sky and Eva began to wonder where Isaac was. When it started to get dark she was really worried about him and talked Nikos into going with her to find him. By the time they found him his leg was swollen and numb and his energy was gone. They unloaded the sled, got Isaac on it and dragged him down to the shop.

Eva ran to get Mother Ruth, who took one look at him and said the leg would have to be set. There was one man in the city with experience in setting bones, and Mother Ruth went after him. It took two men to hold Isaac while he got it set. Isaac passed out with the pain and Eva cried. The bone setter said if it didn't get infected it should be pretty well healed in six weeks or so. Mother Ruth wanted to take Isaac home but it was too far to move him in his condition. Eva decided she would see after him there in the shop.

Isaac's temperature went up, and he got out of his head with fever. Eva kept cool compresses on his forehead and leg, and Mother Ruth brought him a steady diet of broth. After about four days, his temperature was near normal. Another week and Isaac was getting to be a fussy patient, so Eva and Mother Ruth decided he must be getting better. A steady stream of visitors came by, some with food, some with good wishes, and everyone looking at the pottery in the shop. Isaac became the pottery salesman and business was even better than it had been.

It seemed like forever, but finally Mother Ruth and the bone setter said it was time to try his leg. Simon made him some crutches, and after a shaky start, he was moving around in the shop.

Isaac developed a little sales pitch about how sturdy and durable the pottery was, and that it had been fired and was able to withstand the temperatures needed for cooking. He was also sure to show everyone the decorative pottery and statues that could be used for displays and holding flowers, or just to look nice. He soon became a first class salesman with his friendly patter and presentation. Mother Ruth was afraid he might oversell things, and people might end up not being happy with what they brought home, but Nikos said not to worry. If anyone was unhappy with their purchases, they could return them, and he would refund their payment, but no one ever was.

In four more weeks Isaac was walking without crutches but he had a limp that would be with him the rest of his life.

5

ISAAC AND EVA

Isaac felt his life getting more complicated. His dream of learning a trade no longer mattered. Every day but Sabbath was spent in the pottery shop with his new friends, Nikos and Eva. He and Eva had become such good friends; they were like brother and sister. But now he doesn't want Eva to be a sister. He is confused and wants her to be more than a sister. All he can think of is being around her all the time. They talk when they are working, and he has found out that her mother died when she was born and a couple of old aunts had taken care of her when she was small while Nikos was working. When she reached sixteen Nikos decided they needed to get away someplace else, on their own. She was getting older and Nikos didn't want her to end up married to any of the young men from around where they lived. That's why they came to Capernaum. Nikos' friend told him about this beautiful city on the Sea of Galilee, this city and its people, and the thought that it would be a better place to live. She smiled and said she thought Papa's friend was right. She liked it here, and its people.

Isaac took his confusion to Mother Ruth who said, "Isaac, I knew this day would come. You are in love, and your sweetheart is Greek, not Jew, and you have not had a father to guide you. You still want to be a fisherman but you don't want to leave your friends without your help. You must take these problems and work through them. First, have you discussed this with Eva or her father, and do you know how she feels?"

"No," Isaac said.

"Then you must find out how Eva feels about you. Then I will try to be both mother and father to you and guide you in what to do next."

The next day was the Sabbath, Isaac wasn't sleeping, he was lying awake at night thinking of Eva, and he thought of her all day on the Sabbath. That night he was so tired he finally slept, but woke early in the morning and went to the pottery shop where he loaded his clay buckets on the sled.

Just as he was going up the hill Eva came out of the house, still wearing her apron from fixing breakfast; with a smile on her face that melted Isaac she gave him a cheery, "Good morning Isaac."

Isaac felt warm all over, and knew what he had to do. He said, "Come with me to get a load of clay."

She headed back to the house, taking off her apron as she ran, and shouted over her shoulder, "Let me tell Papa, and I will be right back."

Neither said a word as they dragged the sled up the hill to the clay pit. Still in silence, they filled the buckets and then Isaac sat on a log lying next to the clay pit. Still not saying anything, he motioned for Eva to come and sit by him. Finally Isaac broke the silence. "Eva, we need to talk, I love you."

Eva smiled and without hesitation took his arm and said, "Isaac, I love you too."

It was such a relief to Isaac. He put his arm around her and said, "We have much to talk about. First, it is our custom for the parents to arrange for their children's weddings, but you know I am an orphan. The only family I have is Mother Ruth and Simon, and they aren't even blood relatives. Next, you are Greek and I am Jew, and I have no Idea what Nikos will say, when we tell him we are in love.

They sat for a few minutes, Isaac's arm still around Eva, and she had leaned over and put her head on his shoulder. Finally Isaac said, "Mother Ruth is a very good and smart woman. Let's take the clay down the hill and go talk to her.

As soon as they came in the door, Mother Ruth could tell by the look of them that something had happened. "Mother Ruth! Eva and I are in love. What must we do?"

"I will go talk to Nikos," she said. But first, what have you two discussed about your differences in faith?"

"Papa and I have never worshiped any god," Eva said, "And never talked about it. Neither have Isaac and me, except he told me that you worship the one and only true God of Israel, the creator of all things, and that he is a good, loving, and forgiving God. I like that and I wish I were a Jew."

"So!" Mother Ruth said. "I will go talk to Nikos and we will see what we shall see." Then she left with a smile on her face, but saying nothing more; leaving Eva and Isaac to worry and wait.

When Ruth entered the pottery shop Nikos had his pottery wheel spinning, forming a large pot. She wasted no time, but came straight to the point.

"Nikos, we must talk about our children."

Nikos tried to be calm, but his hand slipped and he suddenly had a large blob of clay on his wheel. "I know," said Nikos. "I have watched them as they have fallen in love and probably knew what was happening before they did. I suppose they want to get married."

"They didn't say that, but I am sure it is what they want. What are your feelings, Nikos?"

Nikos looked far away for a few moments before he said, "Ruth, Isaac is a good man. He is a hard worker and says he wants to be a fisherman. I could teach him to be a potter, but that isn't what he wants. The only reason he stays around here is to be near Eva and to help me. I have no doubt that whatever he does he could and would take care of my daughter and support a family. Sooner or later the pottery market is going to catch up and there won't be enough work to support us all. I have worried about Eva for some time. She is of marrying age and Isaac is the only young man I have seen that would make her a good husband. If they want to get married they have my blessing. What do you think Ruth?"

"I feel the same way, except I think they need to work out how they feel and what they want to do about their differences in faith." said Ruth.

Nikos said, "We worship no gods." I have tried to raise Eva to be a good person, loving, and kind, and although I have a vague notion of what it is to be a Jew, I do not know what you believe."

"Eva says she wants to convert to Judaism, but there would be some training and rituals involved." Ruth said.

"Ruth, I think the two of them were made for each other, if you are willing, I would like to give them our blessing," Nikos said.

Mother Ruth said, "Then it is done. Come with me and let's give them our blessing and our best wishes, Nikos."

Isaac and Eva were still sitting on the same bench in Mother Ruth's kitchen; the same place they were when she went to talk to Nikos. Ruth came in the back door, followed by Nikos, and the two of them immediately stood up, red faced and slightly trembling. Eva was holding Isaac's hand with a death grip. Nikos and mother Ruth looked at each other, neither of them speaking, neither wanted to be the first. Finally mother Ruth looked at Nikos and said, "Say something, you are the man. Tell them what we have decided."

Nikos cleared his throat. "We are aware that the two of you are in love, are of marrying age, and would like our blessing. After some discussion we have decided that the two of you should be married and that you have our blessing.

Suddenly there were four sighs of relief, laughter, and a lot of hugging. Tomorrow Isaac would go see the rabbi and they would start making arrangements.

The next morning Isaac went to see Rabbi Levi. When he found him he was working on the door of the synagogue. "It doesn't close properly," said Rabbi Levy, "and when it rains water pours in." Isaac helped him and they had it repaired in no time. Then the rabbi said, "I appreciate your help in repairing this door, although I doubt that that is why you came to see me Alph. How can I help you?"

Isaac told him he had met a girl, she was Greek, and he wanted to marry her.

"That is no secret, Isaac. Everyone in town knows of you and Eva, that you are in love and don't know what to do about it. We have all been guessing when you would figure it out. Ever since your family was killed in that boat accident everyone in town has tried to kind of look after you. We are all your family. We were thrilled when you returned from Egypt and told all of your experiences and we are all thrilled that you are now a man and about to be married. We have also gotten to know Eva and love her also. She does not have to convert to Judaism for marriage to you although it would probably strengthen your marriage and be better for your children. It mostly depends on how Eva feels about conversion."

"She wants to," said Isaac. "She is going to live with mother Ruth and I am going to live with Nikos until we are married."

"Ruth knows the Torah very well." Said Rabbi Levy, "and she can teach Eva our history, our customs, and about God. Eva will become a Ger, a stranger or sojourner living in our community. Remember, the Lord said that we were strangers while we were living in Egypt. She will be a non-Jewish inhabitant of the land of Israel who observes the seven laws of Noah and repudiates all links with idolatry. We will give her a ritual bath, and she will become a Jew by conversion. Then we will love her as we love ourselves."

So, Eva and Nikolas both studied and converted to Judaism. Eva took her ritual bath, Nikos went through the circumcision, and they both became Jews.

Isaac and Eva were married and moved into Isaac's old home next door to Mother Ruth. They continued working in the pottery shop, and Isaac became like a son to Nikos. In fact, they call each other Papa and son. Eva began calling Mother Ruth just Mother but to Isaac, even though he loved her as a mother, she was his Mother Ruth.

6

ISAAC'S NEW JOB

S everal months passed as Isaac and Ruth settled into their new home together. Eva was so busy making her nest for Isaac and herself that she no longer went to the pottery shop. Nikos and Isaac seemed to be doing very well alone, so she worked at home, popping over to Mother's two or three times a day for help, advice, or just to talk. All was well with the world and everyone was happy.

Happy, that is, until Nikos stopped him one day just as he was leaving for home. "My son Nikos said. I have some bad news for you. I am afraid the pottery shop is not going to provide for all of us for very many more months. We are no longer getting many new customers. I had counted on merchants from other cities coming over to buy goods to sell in their shops, but it just isn't happening, and our retail market here is just about saturated. We will continue to get sales from our old customers but only to replace broken items or for gifts. You have said you would like to be a fisherman. This might be a good time for you to look seriously at it. I can support us by myself for a while, while you get started in business, but I am afraid it can't last."

Isaac took a slow sad walk home. Eva met him with a smile and a big hug. "I have something to tell you. You are going to be a Papa."

"Isaac! Eva shouted. You are supposed to be happy."

"I am!" he exclaimed. "It's just that......and then his voice trailed off, and he told Eva everything Nikos had told him."

Eva looked at Isaac seriously. What do you think our savings are for? There is enough for a baby and enough for you to start a business."

"But Eva," Isaac said, "That money is supposed to be for emergencies."

"What do you think emergencies are? This is an emergency."

He smiled and held her tight for a long time.

The next morning Isaac went by the pottery shop and told Nikos he was going job hunting.

Then he walked down to the dock to hunt his friend David, where he found him loading his nets into the boat. Isaac put on his best face and with a big smile said, "Good morning. David. How is the fishing going?"

David sat on the dock support by his boat and said, "Not too well my friend. My father's joints are swollen and painful. Some days he can't even go out to fish, and some of our fishing hands have quit to go find better work. Our business may collapse"

Then Isaac told David what was happening to his father-in-law's pottery business. "I have to find something else, and quick." He said. "Eva is expecting a baby in a few months, so I have another mouth to feed."

"I understand." said David. "We have two boys to feed, clothe, and care for."

"How much would it cost for me to buy a partnership with you and take your father's place?" Isaac said to David.

David's countenance brightened and he thought for a few moments before answering. "I think half of our boat and equipment and business should be worth about three denarii, but I will have to speak to my father."

Denarii was said to be worth ten asses. That would be thirty asses for half of the fishing business. Isaac knew that the business established by David's father was good. They had a nice boat that would easily carry an eight man crew and some fine nets. Their buckets and small equipment were all good and they had a fine business reputation, but still.....thirty assess was a lot for half of a floundering business, even though it did have a good reputation.

Isaac said, "We don't have enough in our savings to pay you that much, but we could raise two denarii.

David said, "I will speak to my father."

Isaac returned home and asked for a family meeting. He recounted the conversation with David. He said, "Three denarii would take all of our savings and I am not comfortable with doing that."

Nikos and Mother Ruth both said they could give them some money if they needed it.

"Well then," Isaac said, "I will talk to David tomorrow and if he asks more than two denarii, I will return with his offer before I close a deal."

In the morning, Isaac was at the dock early. He could tell nothing from the expression on David's face when he arrived. So he said, "What did your father say, David?"

My father says we can accept your two denarii offer, but if you try it and want out, we can give you back only half of what we get when we sell the business."

"That would be fair, my friend," said Isaac. But, if I commit to a partnership I will not back out. I will meet you with the money in the morning and we will go fishing."

"There were no papers to sign, no oaths to swear, and nothing to be recorded any place. There were however several men on the dock who had heard the transaction. That was enough. David and Isaac were partners."

"In the morning," said David.

"In the morning," replied Isaac, and they each left for home.

When Isaac got back to the house, Eva was busy with her chores.

"Eva," shouted Isaac. "I'm a fisherman."

Eva came into the room with her hands on her hips and a scowl on her face. "I suppose this means you will be coming home smelling like fish every day."

Isaac was startled until she started laughing and poked him in the ribs.

"You are going to be a wonderful fisherman," she said. "When do you start?"

"In the morning," he said, and they grabbed each other in one of their long hugs.

Isaac got out their money and tied it in a cloth to take to David the next day while Eva made a big dinner for them.

Later, Isaac rolled onto his bed and thought about the lives of him and David. When he was young he was David's little tag along friend. David took care of Isaac, looked after him and helped him grow up. He was David's student in life in many ways. He had taught him to swim, taught him about girls, and gave him some good advice as he grew into being a man. He had a lot to be thankful for, for David being such a good friend. When Isaac returned from Egypt David had gone into business with his father but now Isaac was grown, married, about to be a father and he and David were going to be business partners. He was looking forward to maybe a lifetime of their working together.

Isaac relaxed and slept better that night than he had in days, or at least since Nikos had given him the bad news about the decline in the pottery business.

The next morning, Isaac handed David his money. David said, "I will take this to father and be right back."

For the next few minutes Isaac checked their nets and looked over their boat. It was a big boat, obviously big enough for an eight man crew, maybe ten if you crowded just a little. One man would have a difficult time rowing and maneuvering it, but two men could handle it at a very low speed.

When David returned they decided to go out onto the lake and cast a net, just to see if they could catch anything on their first run. With David on the right and Isaac on the left they headed out for deep water. They'd rowed for about tem minutes when they noticed the sky getting dark. They looked behind them and saw a black cloud coming down from the mountains, headed straight for the Sea of Galilee. The men on the dock were waving and yelling to them, but they couldn't hear. The wind had picked up and the white caps were starting to appear on the waves. They got the boat turned round but hadn't gone far before the waves were so big they were coming over the sides of the boat. Water began to fill the bottom of the boat and David stripped off his clothes and went over the side. Isaac put an oar in the water so he could steer with one arm while dipping water with the other. After a few minutes, it was evident they were making no headway against the wind. Isaac removed his clothes and went over the other side to help David pull the boat. They were holding to the boat with one arm and swimming with the other.

David shouted over the wind, "We will never make it back like this. We have to abandon the boat and swim for our lives.

They made it part way to the dock when the wind stopped blowing and it became easier to swim. The men on the dock were still shouting when they pulled themselves up on the dock. They were saying, "Look at your boat!" It was still floating, with just the top rail sticking out of the water. The wind had died just in time to keep it from sinking.

One of the other fishing crews took them out to their boat, and another came out to help dip water. After a lot of bailing they towed it back to the fishing dock. Thankful and exhausted, they tied up their boat and went home.

The story of their first day together as a fishing crew would be told for long time; almost as long as the story to Egypt and back.

When Eva heard of Isaac and David's experience she was greatly concerned. In fact she was more than greatly concerned. All she could think of was what had happened to Isaac's parents and sister in their boating accident, and what could have happened to him. By the time she heard the entire story she was crying.

"I don't want to be left a widow to raise our child by myself," she told Isaac.

He promised; it will never happen again.

She said, "It had better not. When the weather is bad, I want you here in the house with me."

"I will be," he said, and hugged her tightly. "I promise you, I will be here with you."

The next morning, Isaac and David met at the dock. They agreed it was foolish to go out in the boat, regardless of weather, with less than four men. It just isn't safe business. In fact, six men would be even better, and with clear skies.

Now they needed some fishermen to work for them, in spite of the previous day's escapade. Two of the men who worked for David's father agreed to work for them the first day, knowing that their pay would depend on the number of fish they caught. By mid-morning they were out on the lake, and by noon their nets were full. They rowed their boat to the unloading dock at the fish market. They settled up with the buyer and found they had enough money to pay their fishing hands for the whole week. All of this was new to Isaac, but he loved every minute of it. By the end of the first month they had a full crew and were on their way to operating a profitable business.

7

ALP AND RUTH REACH A LIFE CHANGE

Time was getting close for the arrival of the baby. Mother Ruth insisted that Eva spend most of her days resting while she did the cooking and most of the household chores. It didn't seem like the baby would ever come, and then one afternoon it was time. Mother Ruth put Eva in bed and then started out the door to get Nikos. On the way she saw Isaac coming up from the dock.

"Isaac," she shouted, "Go get the mid-wife, it is time!"

Isaac ran as fast as his weak leg would carry him. The mid-wife wasn't home. Her family said she was gone to the market. Isaac looked in three shops before he found her.

He took the packages she had purchased and said, "It is time for our baby. Go to my house, and I will take your packages home."

Isaac delivered the packages she had purchased and told the mid-wife's family she was at his house helping with the baby. He then flew home with the urgency of a new father.

Mother Ruth met him at the door and told him, "Go get Nikos, and tell him I said he was to come and keep you company. Then the two of you can sit outside on the benches until I call you."

Nikos was making a pot when Isaac came in. He didn't have to say a word. The expression on Isaac's face told him all he needed to know. He dropped his work and the two of them hurried to the benches in front of the house, to do nothing until they were called. The women had been working on names for several weeks. If it was a girl Eva wanted her to be called Ruth, but a boy wasn't so easy for her to decide. He could be Nikos, or named after his father or his other grandfather. Eva liked John Mark. No one I the family had that name, she just thought it a good name.

An hour went by; and then two; and then three. Isaac was getting nervous. This was his first child. Nikos was getting nervous. This was his first grandchild. What could be wrong? Then he remembered he forgot to tell Simon. There were some boys playing in the street. He fished in his pockets and found a coin and gave it to one of the boys. He told him to go tell Simon, the carpenter, that the baby was coming.

The boys started running and within a few minutes Simon came running.

He wheeled around and said, "I forgot something; and headed back home.

In a few minutes he was back carrying a large beautiful cradle. He said, "Eva will need this. I finished it a few weeks ago, but waited. I wanted to wait and let it be it to be a surprise."

At this point it was hard to say which was the most nervous; father, grandfather, or uncle, but finally, at the end of the fifth hour, they heard a baby's cry.

They whooped and hollered, and several of the neighbors heard what was happening and joined the party.

Mother Ruth came out and said, "Isaac, you are a father. It's a boy!"

"What's his name," asked Nikos?

"He won't be named until the Bris said Isaac, but it will be, "Alph."

The entire community knew the story of the Egyptian trip and the name, "Alph."

Time flew by. Alph was properly named at his Bris, and it seemed no time until he began to walk. This didn't mean that Eva was without problems, for now she had four boys to take care of for almost every evening meal, they were attended by the whole crowd. It was as if she and Mother Ruth were cooking for some kind of eatery. There was Alph, father Isaac, Grandfather Nikos, and Uncle Simon, as well as Mother Ruth and Eva.

Overnight she went from being wife for two, to caregiver for a family of seven, but she didn't seem to mind. In fact, over the years, as the family grew, Eva's table became the family's meeting place for dinner, for news, problem solving and planning. And, everyone brought pots of stew, bread, bowls of fruit, and whatever else they could work in.

Before long Grandpa Nikos started taking time off from his work during the day, to give Eva a rest. When the weather was right he would take Alph all over town, visiting shops, the market, his friends or anyone they happened to meet on the street. By the time he was two everyone along their visiting route knew Alph. He would hold one of Grandpa's fingers and toddle along beside him. When Alph got tired Grandpa would carry him and when Grandpa got tired they went home. They almost always went by Simon's wood-shop and, if it wasn't too late, would try to catch Papa coming up from his boat to walk home with them.

In the spring, Grandmother Ruth got ready to plant her garden. She turned the soil and then took a stick and made rows. Alph helped by planting the seed. Some seeds were barely covered with dirt and others were buried over an inch deep, but it didn't seem to matter, they all seemed to grow anyway. Alph delighted in pulling weeds out of the garden, but sometimes got mixed up on weeds and good plants. Nikos made him a little jar and it was one plant, one jar of water. They all got their share. When the fall harvest arrived he had to be watched closely or everything would be harvested, green or ripe.

Alph turned four and family life was going smoothly. The fishing business was going good and pottery sales had picked up so much that Nikos had to take orders. He couldn't keep his shelves stocked. Eva and Mother Ruth had started coming over and lending a hand. Summer had come and gone and the early fall weather was beautiful. This year Alph had learned to tell green from ripe.

One evening, Eva walked down to the dock to meet Isaac as he, David and the crew came in with a large catch of fish. Isaac waved and shouted that he would join her as soon as the boat was unloaded. David said, "Go join your wife; we will unload for you today. I will see you in the morning."

Isaac went over and risked a public display of affection by giving her a big hug, a smelly big hug of freshly caught fish, but she didn't seem to mind.

"It's good to have you meet me." Isaac said, "But why are you here today?"

"We need to talk," She said. "I have some news for you and didn't want anyone else to know before you."

Isaac became concerned, "What is it?" he asked.

Eva smiled and said, "You are going to be a father again."

This time Isaac lifted her off of her feet, swung her around, and shouted so that everyone on the dock could hear, "I'm going to be a father again."

Shouts of congratulations came from the small crowd as Isaac and Eva went home to tell the family.

They waited until everyone was there at the evening meal to announce the news. Everyone but Alph was delighted. He couldn't understand what was happening.

Isaac said, "Alph, you are going to have a little brother or sister."

"You mean, like Timothy?" Alf asked

Timothy was the friend Alf played with every day. And who had a baby sister named Sarah. So Alph started running in circles Shouting, "Yay-ay-ay-ay-ay."

It seemed joy had spread to everyone.

Alph wanted to know when the baby was coming. Where was it coming from? If it wasn't going to come very soon, maybe he and Grandpa could go get it? It seemed he asked a hundred questions every day about the baby. Time went by, and the questions diminished. Alph and Grandpa spent more time together so Eva could rest. Sometimes they went for a walk and sometimes Alph just hung around the pottery shop, while Grandpa made pots. Sometimes Grandpa would give him a lump of wet clay, and he could make things out of it, usually a plate for his mother or the new baby.

One morning Isaac woke Alph early. It was just turning daylight. The sun wasn't even up yet. Alph wanted to know why Papa was getting him up so early. Isaac told him it was because he was going over to Grandpa's for the day, while the baby came.

"No," Alph said. "I want to stay and meet the baby."

But, there was no arguing with Papa, who finished getting him breakfast, and rushed him off to Grandpa's. As they left, Grandmother Ruth and a strange lady arrived.

"Who's that?" Alph wanted to know.

"It's just a friend. Coming to see Mother," Isaac said." She will be gone by the time you come home."

By that point, they were across the street at Grandpa's house. It would be nice to say it was planned, but it wasn't. It just happened that it was Alph's fifth birthday. The day went by. Alph took a nap, and when he woke up his uncle Simon was there with Grandpa.

Alph's eyes were still full of sleep, but he quickly remembered why he was at Grandpa's, and he wanted to know if the new baby was there yet.

"Not yet," said Grandpa. "But it won't be long."

Nikos and Simon were as anxious as Alph. Every few minutes one of them peered out the door to see if anyone was coming.

Suddenly, Isaac was there, swooping Alph up in his arms and saying, "Come on Alph, you and your Grandpa, and Uncle Simon, need to come and see your new sister; her name is Ruth.

"But that's Grandmother's name," Alph said.

"Yes it is," Isaac agreed, "We named her after her grandmother."

"But that's my grandmother, Alph said.

"Yes I know," explained Isaac, "She is your grandmother and she's Ruth's grandmother. Just like I'm your Papa and her Papa, mother is your mother and her mother too."

"Why?" Alph asked.

"It's because you are brother and sister. You have the same mother and the same father, and the same grandfather and the same Uncle Simon."

Alph said, "Okay," although he didn't really understand.

And then Isaac said, "You also have the same birthday, but you are five years older than she is."

"Is that because she is my sister?"

"No," Isaac said, "That part just happened.

That didn't make sense to Alph, but he couldn't think of any more questions, so he just stayed quiet. He would work on it later.

When they came in, baby Ruth was asleep in her cradle, the same cradle that was Alph's when he was a baby.

Alph beamed when he saw her. "That's my baby sister. Can she come out and play with me?"

"It will be a little while before she is big enough," Said Grandmother. "You will have to wait until she is a little bigger."

Grow she did, and it was no time until she was crawling everywhere. She and Alph bonded quickly. He would sit in his little chair that uncle Simon had made him and hold her and talk to her, and she would listen to everything he said. She watched everything he did too. When she started to talk, the first word she said was, "Alph." When she was fussy, Eva could put her in Alph's lap, and she would quiet down and go right to sleep. For a while Alph was the only one who could understand her baby gibberish. They had their own language and Alph would translate what she was saying.

By the time Ruth was two, Alph would take her outside for a walk like Grandpa did him, except it was a shorter route. It included Grandma's house, the pottery shop, and Simon's wood shop unless Grandpa was along, and then they would go everywhere Grandpa would take them.

8

SIMON'S TRIP

One evening, after dinner, Isaac and Simon were sitting on the bench in front of the house talking. Simon said, "Isaac, I'm going to Jericho tomorrow for some hardware. I will probably be gone about a week, if you would keep an eye on my shop.

"Well, I always do, "Isaac replied.

"I know, and I go there two or three times a year for metal fasteners, nails and hinges, but this time there is something else." He looked down the road and rubbed his hands together. "When Anna died, I didn't think I ever wanted to marry again. But I'm having second thoughts now. It's been eighteen years since that boating accident took my sweetheart, and I've thought of Anna and missed her every day. It's been lonely." He glanced over at Isaac before he continued.

"The blacksmith I buy my parts from has a daughter named Mary, who works in his store. She is twenty eight and never married. She is pretty, but very shy, and has pulled back from any young men who have tried to be friendly with her. Her father told me he didn't think she would ever marry. She has gotten past the marrying age, but she and I have gotten to be good friends over the years that I have been doing business with her father. She told me she is a younger cousin to David, your fishing partner. They are going to move to Capernaum and I don't know what to do. I am comfortable in being friends with Mary, but if she moves here, what will our friendship become. I feel like I will be unfaithful to Anna if I pursue a romance with her."

Isaac sat in silence as Simon told his story. Then he said, "Simon, if you had died instead of Anna, wouldn't you have wanted Anna to have pursued a new life? Life can be lonely without a partner. I think Anna would want you to pursue a new life. I have wondered many times why you have not remarried. I was pretty young when Anna died, but as brother and sister we were very close. She would talk to me like I was her age, and I think I knew her very well. I know she loved you dearly, but out of that love I know she would want you to be happy if she had to leave you, and she did. It has been your choice and I have never wanted to press you. Anna was my sister and you have been my brother all these years. I would like to see you do what is best for you. Maybe it's time. Mary is older than most girls when they marry, but then so are you. But you aren't that ancient. You are both still young enough to raise a family."

"Thank you, Isaac. I just wanted to know how you would feel should anything happen."

"You have done much for me over the years and are the only brother I have," said Isaac. "Anything that makes you happy will make me happy too."

The next morning Simon went to the pottery shop and asked Nikos if he could barrow Plato and his cart for a trip to Jericho. Nikos was happy for Simon to take Plato on a trip. He hadn't had him out in quite a while and he was getting fat and lazy.

Simon thanked him and said he would take good care of him. He harnessed the donkey and took him over to the carpenter shop. It only took him a few minutes to grease the cart's wheels, load food for him and Plato, extra clothes, a goatskin of water, and they were on the road to Jericho.

Simon traveled out to the edge of town where the road starts to wind down into the Jordan Valley. He stopped in a little gathering area where travelers gather before they start their journey. Robbers or wild animals can be a problem to very small groups or people traveling alone, so, most people gather here and wait until there is a group who can travel together. This morning there was a family there who Simon knew, the man's name was Bartholomew with his wife and three good sized boys.

"Good morning," Simon said, "are you waiting on a group to travel?"

"Yes" said the man, "But I think we are probably okay with who we have now."

"I think so," said Simon, "I think the two of us and those three boys of yours will make safe travel, if you're comfortable with it."

"I am," he said. "Where are you going?"

"Jericho," Simon said, I'm going down to pick up some metalwork for my shop."

"We're going to Jerusalem for a family visit," said Bartholomew, "We can travel together as far as Jericho and will have no problem going up the mountain. That road is heavily traveled."

And so, the little crowd of six began their journey.

Simon had told Isaac and Nikos he would be back in about a week, but when he hadn't returned in two weeks they began to worry about him. After twenty-five days it was time to do something. They decided that in the morning they would see if they could get one or two volunteers to go with them to find out what had happened to Simon.

Just after sundown that same evening however Simon and two other people arrived, tired and dusty from their trip. Even poor Plato was tired. Everyone gathered around and Simon introduced Mary, his new wife, and Daniel, his father-in-law. The only one who wasn't really surprised was Isaac. He had been wondering if Mary had not been the reason he was gone so long. He looked at Simon and gave him a smile and a wink.

Nikos, Simon, and Isaac took the cart to Simon's shop and unloaded it. The cart was so full of personal items they had to tie them on to keep them from falling off on the trip. The men kept asking questions but Simon said, "Wait until we get everyone together or I will be telling my story over and over. When they finished emptying the cart Isaac took Plato to his little home, and gave him a well-deserved rubdown, and went back to his home. Grandmother Ruth had prepared some food for them, and while they ate Simon told this story.

"The first evening I was in Jericho Mary invited me to dinner. Daniel went to bed after dinner, and Mary and I sat up and talked late into the night. Mary said her mother had died five years earlier, and she stayed with her father, keeping house and working in the store. Her father is a smithy and had a shop and forge behind the store, and they lived in quarters above the store. Work had been slow this past year, and Daniel started talking about moving to Capernaum, and starting a metal shop there. The trade caravans come through Capernaum and he can buy raw metal from them and sell his finished products back to them. Metal shops in Jerusalem took most of the work in the area and he thought that Capernaum might give him more business than the shop in Jericho."

" I felt attracted to Mary the first time we met, but that night as she told her story I felt even much more attracted to her. She asked about my family and I told her I had no blood related family but had all of you. I told her about losing Anna eighteen years ago and about Isaac and Eva, about Mother Ruth, and Nikos, and Alph and how Alph liked hanging around the wood shop and about little Ruth, and most of all how much I love all of you. I told her that you are my family and I wouldn't dream of living anyplace else. Business is good, and Capernaum is just a great place to be. I told her about Isaac's trip to Egypt and how interesting it was to hear of his adventures, and how Isaac and David almost lost their boat on their first day as partners."

"I asked Mary when she thought they would move and she said probably soon."

"The next day I picked out the materials I wanted and loaded them on the cart, but put off making preparation to leave, because Mary encouraged me to stay. It didn't take much encouragement. After a couple more days visiting with her, we began to talk about a life together. We went to Daniel, and he gave us his blessing. It was settled. We were married there in Jericho, and Daniel began making plans for moving to Capernaum."

"For the next week and a half, all three of us worked at separating the things they needed and those they could afford to leave behind. We decided that if all three of us walked and helped the little donkey by pushing the cart up hills, we could make Capernaum in about five days. Daniel knew a man who was interested in his shop and had no trouble selling it, and soon we were on our way."

Then Simon said, "That is pretty much our story. Mary and I really love each other, and I'm glad I brought her into the family. As you get to know, you will too. She is kind, gentle, and sweet. I can't believe I have been this lucky twice in my life."

By now it was late, but Alph had been awake through the whole story and wanted to know who Daniel and Mary were to him.

"Mary is your aunt," Simon said, "because she is my wife. Aunts and uncles go together. We are your Uncle Simon and Aunt Mary. Daniel could be a grandfather, and then you would have two grandfathers. We will have to see what Daniel and Grandpa think tomorrow.

Alph scratched his head as he wandered off to bed, wondering how these new people were going to affect him. Daniel went home with Nikos and Mary went with Simon to try her first night in her new home.

Morning came and Alph was ready for a better explanation about these people. Grandpa explained to him, "Mary is like what Uncle Simon said last night. She is your aunt because she is Simon's wife. They are Aunt Mary and Uncle Simon.

As soon as he saw her Alph had to try it out. He said, "Hi Aunt Mary."

Mary blushed and then said, "Hi Alph."

Alph smiled. That worked. Now what should he do about Daniel. He had to figure out what to call him. Nikos and Daniel tried some titles.

Finally Nikos said, "Why don't you call him Grandfather and you call me Grandpa and then you will have a Grandpa and a Grandfather."

Alph thought that was good, so he tied it out. "Hi Grandfather."

Daniel was pleased to finally have a grandchild. He grabbed Alph and hugged him and said, "Hi Alph."

Everyone was happy with the new names, and Alph could hardly wait for papa to get home from fishing so he could tell him.

That evening the men sat on the benches in front of the house to talk and relax. Alph came out and joined them. He said, "Papa I have a new aunt and a new grandfather. Uncle Simon's new wife is my Aunt Mary and I call my new grandfather, Grandfather."

Isaac laughed and picked Alph up and said, "Alph, our family is growing," with a new aunt and a new grandfather."

"Yes," said Alph, as he swung on his Papa's arm and dropped to the ground to run off and play with Timothy.

Isaac stoked his beard. "We need to talk about more permanent living arrangements." Then he laughed and said, "This family almost needs a hotel."

Nikos grinned and said, "Daniel and I already have it worked out. He is going to take Eva's old room and my shop area is more than big enough for the both of us. He is going to put his forge next to my kiln and we can share the same firewood pile. We will do fine. We may even put a sign over our business, "Two Grandfathers, Metal and Pottery."

Simon laughed and said, "The sign will almost be bigger than the businesses. Mary and I will be fine. I built our house for a family, and now we are a family, with plenty of room."

"I have talked to Mother Ruth about and idea I have," said Isaac. "There is an empty space between her house and ours, with enough space to build a room for Alph, one for Little Ruth, and a passage way to Mother Ruth's house. Most of the time, we all eat together in the evening, and we would have more room for family time together. Also, I have always wanted a stairway to the roof so we could sleep up there when the weather was nice." And then he laughed and said, "We could call it "The Hotel."

"If we are going to take on this project," said Nikos, "we had better get started before the cool, rainy season sets in. If we wait too long, Isaac will have a whole city designed for us to build."

After some discussion with the women on what they wanted, the project was started. Between their jobs, Nikos and Daniel hauled basalt blocks from the mine in the hills up the Jordan River, Simon stockpiled wood for the frame and Isaac, with Plato's help hauled the clay they would need to make their mud. It took a couple of months to get all of their material together. They day the construction started, David, the men who worked for him and Isaac, and even some of the neighbors joined in. It was all that Eva, Mother Ruth, and Mary could do to keep a food supply for the workers going, and keep Alph and little Ruth out of their way. In a week the job was done, and there was even a stairway up the back of the house, off limits to Little Ruth without an adult with her, and roof access for Isaac's warm summer night sleeping.

This new construction completed one long U shaped house, from the east side of Isaac and Eva's house, to the far west of Simon's wood shop. Everyone had their own private space, but they were all together under one roof.

There was a courtyard, in the open area of the U shaped building, and they paved it with basalt blocks, except for Mother Ruth's garden, and a room with one side open for storing firewood and doing laundry. Plato and the two grandfathers were across the street and they said they needed that space for peace and quiet.

On bath nights it was Alph's job to bathe his little sister, tuck her into bed, and tell her a story. Then, he could take his own bath, and if the weather was right, carry his bed matt up on the roof and sleep under the stars. Across the street, where Plato and the two grandfathers lived, it was quiet and peaceful, both day and night, unless they were on babysitting duty.

Plato had a large pen that housed the kiln and forge, and bordered one side of their building. Sometimes he stood and watched them fire their forge or kiln, or if they were working inside, he would stand with his head in the window watching what was going on. Other times he stood by his front fence watching the house across the street. If the children were out and saw him they would go over and play with him, ride on him or come up to the fence and scratch his head and back. When Eva's work was caught up she would come out and sit on the benches or walk over and talk to Plato. Women going to or from the market would often stop at the benches and visit with Eva, and Plato would stand by the fence and watch them. If no one was outside, or he could see no one through the window, Plato would show his impatience to a lack of company by standing by the fence and braying loudly. And, he wouldn't quit until someone came and paid him some attention.

9

PLAYTIME TURNS TO LEARNING

Jewish law says "Remember the days of old, consider the years long past; ask your father and he will inform you; your elders and they will tell you." It also says: "keep these words that I am commanding you today in your heart. Recite them to your children and talk about them when you are at home and when you are away, when you lie down, and when you rise. Bind them as a sign on your hand, fix them as an emblem on your forehead, and write them on the doorposts of your house and on your gates."

When Alph was born, Isaac remembered how his teaching had been neglected after he became an orphan. He didn't want Alph to experience that and he wrote those words on the doorposts of their house and on their gate just as the law instructed.

Isaac had been teaching Alph a little at a time ever since, but now he was seven, He should have started school a year earlier, but Isaac had been preoccupied with all that was going on in the family. Now it was time for a more formal education, where Alph could not only learn more of the Torah, but could also learn his numbers, reading, and writing. He began attending the rabbi's daily classes, learning the Mishnah. When he was thirteen he would have his bar mitzvah and take on the moral responsibilities of and adult Jew. These subjects are pretty heavy for a boy but necessary to prepare him for the adult life of a devout Jew. Alph would still have time to play and be a boy, but his time for playing all day with few responsibilities was over.

He liked doing numbers and reading, but he loved doing anything with his hands. Uncle Simon's carpenter shop held a fascination for him. If he didn't come straight home from school, his Mother knew where she could find him. If he were there too long she would send Little Ruth to tell him to come home. He knew if he didn't come pretty quickly, Mother would come in the door with her hands on her hips, and that spelled trouble.

Uncle Simon started him with a few simple tools so that he could build some things. Within a year, Alph was familiar with every tool in the shop and could use most of them. Uncle Simon was a good teacher, and carpentry was a subject Alph liked. There weren't many eight-year-old boys who could use tools the way Alph could.

One day, Uncle Simon finished a job and had a board almost a cubit long and a half cubit wide left over. Alph's eyes got big. He could just see a small table for mother's kitchen in the board. He asked Uncle Simon if he could have it.

"What do you want with it?" Uncle Simon asked.

When Alph told him his idea, Uncle Simon thought maybe that would just be a good project for him.

One end of the board was jagged, and the other end had been cut at an angle. So, Alph decided the ends should be oval to get the most out of the board. Alph started working on the corners with a draw knife, and little by little it began to rake shape. The work went slowly, but every day he came and worked on it for a while before going home to dinner. He found a place to hide it when he wasn't working on it, in case Mother came into the shop. Of course Aunt Mary was in and out all of the time, so he had to swear her to secrecy. Uncle Simon smiled as he worked, but let him be his own boss, and never said a word unless Alph asked for advice. After a couple of weeks, Alph had his table top shaped and smoothed just like he wanted it. To that point he knew just what he wanted to do, but now it was time for something he knew nothing about, table legs. Alph went to Uncle Simon and asked him how he could make legs.

The first thing Uncle Simon asked was, "How tall do you want the table?"

"I don't know. How tall should it be?"

"Well, if you make it too tall it won't be very stable. But if you make it too short, it won't be very handy to use."

He held his hand a little way above his knee and said, "I'd say about this high is good."

Alph thought that would be a good height, and then started looking for scraps to make the legs.

Simon pulled some pieces of oak tree limbs out of his wood pile, looked at them and said, "How about these?"

Alph was sure they would be just right. Now he needed to clean off all the bark and smooth them up. It turned into quite a job. It took a lot of work with a draw knife and a pumice rock to get them smooth. Just when he thought he had gotten them just right, Uncle Simon would point out some places that needed more work.

Finally, he had them finished. Now, how would he attach them to the top? Uncle Simon showed him how to bore holes in the bottom of the top. Alph would have to be careful. The holes had to be straight, and if they were too deep, they would break through the top and ruin it. It seemed that the farther Alph went with his project, the more difficult it became. One hole every evening was the best he could do. Finally, the holes were finished, He tried the legs, and much to his disappointment the legs were too big to fit the holes. Sad-faced he went to Uncle Simon.

Uncle Simon just laughed and said, "That's the way they are supposed to be, Alph. Now you carefully work down one end of each leg until they just fit into the holes.

So, it was back to work on the legs. After another whole week, the legs were finished. Alph put the legs in the holes in the bottom of the top, and for the first time saw his table standing up. Oh, but there was still a problem. When he picked the table up, the legs fell out.

"What do I do now, Uncle Simon?" He was a little perturbed.

Uncle Simon got a large cup full of gold-colored little chunks of something and said, "You use this."

Alph looked quizzically at the stuff. "What is it?"

"It's animal glue," Uncle Simon said. "We will put a little bit of it in a pot, with a little water, heat it over a fire until it melts, and then put it on the legs. Then we will quickly put the legs in the holes you made, before the glue hardens again."

Alph had never seen Uncle Simon do that, and it almost seemed like magic.

Alph again tried the table after the legs were glued and set. This time it worked much better, except the table was a little wobbly. Uncle Simon assured him that this was not a problem. The legs were not all exactly the same length. He showed Alph how to use the pumice stone to sand the ends of the longest legs until finally all the wobble was out of the table. The table was finished. It came out just like Alph had seen it in his mind, weeks before.

Uncle Simon walked around the table with his chin in his hands, nodding and making sounds of approval.

"Alph," he said, "you have done a beautiful job. There is only one thing you lack. It needs a finish."

"What is that?"

"You must take some sheep oil and a rag," Uncle Simon said. "And rub the table top and legs until they shine. Then you will have an exquisite piece of furniture."

All that was left now was the presentation. Mary and Simon were not about to miss it, and Alph wanted everyone to be there. It would have to be at the evening meal. Mary would set it up. She would make a special pot of mutton stew, and make sure everyone was there for an evening get-together. When Eva asked her why she wanted to do it, Mary just said she wanted to host a meal.

The big day came and Alph was nervous. They decided that Uncle Simon would come last and set the little table just outside the door where Alph could step out and get it when it was time.

Everyone gathered at the dinner table, and as soon as the last person was seated, Alph said, "Mother, I have a surprise for you."

With that, he stepped outside and brought the table in.

Mother gasped. "Alph, that is beautiful! Where did you get it?"

"I made it just for you, for your kitchen." Alph grinned.

Mother started to cry and then Grandmother did, followed by Aunt Mary. Little Ruth didn't understand why everyone was unhappy, so she started crying. Suddenly Alph felt like crying, too.

Uncle Simon held up his hand and said, "It's true. He made every bit of it. I was only an advisor.

Grandpa Nikos was too choked up to say anything.

All Isaac could do was say, "Son we are so proud of you."

"This is too good to go in my kitchen," Mother said. "It goes in our family room to hold flowers and what knots."

The day would be one of those special days remembered in family history.

Even before Alph was born, Isaac had dreamed of having a son who would follow in his footsteps and take over the family business, just as his partner, David, had done with his father and just as David's sons were planning to do. Now this day of family tradition didn't seem like a good idea. He remembered his father having been a fisherman, but now he began to wonder if his dream of becoming a fisherman was because his father was a fisherman or was it just because he liked fishing. This was something he was truly going to have to consider, not for his sake but for Alph's. He was realizing that the teaching of one's child, of guiding him into his adult life, was an overwhelming responsibility.

Before bedtime, Isaac told Alph he wanted him to go out with him in the morning. "It isn't a school day, and it's time you spent a day with me on the boat."

In the morning Alph awoke to Papa's prodding for him to get up. It was time to go to work. Mother fixed them a lunch while they dressed and ate breakfast.

Down at the dock, the men were already loading the nets and oars into the boat. Papa found him a place to sit where he wouldn't be in the way, and they started out to sea. All morning they dragged the nets through the water but gathered only a handful of fish. Not long after lunch there was a big jerk on the nets and Alph could feel the boat pulling over to the load. Everyone was suddenly busy with their job. The men secured the nets and began rowing for all they were worth toward the fishing dock.

They were in luck and didn't have to wait for someone else to finish unloading. They tied the boat up beside the fish tank, and the men got out their buckets and started unloading, being careful that the counter could see every fish being unloaded into the tank. Today they would finish early and be home before dark.

Isaac had watched Alph all day. He had looked bored in the morning when there were no fish, but so was everyone else. In the afternoon, once they caught some fish, Alph was all eyes as the men rolled the nets over their catch of fish and secured them. Then it was like a race, as every oar was pulled hard to get them into port. How do you tell the level of excitement of a boy on his first commercial fishing day? Isaac wondered. It will take many more trips and getting him into the work to see if he really likes it.

10

ALPH BECOMES A MAN

When a Jewish boy becomes old enough to be responsible for his actions, he becomes a bar mitzvah. On the first Sabbath of his fourteenth year, Alph was called up to read from the weekly portion of the Torah and to recite the benediction. Everyone in the family was invited afterward to his celebration party, and the rabbi gave him a special blessing. Officially Alph was now a man. It was time to change his routine. He began working with Papa and David's fishing crew every day, but it was not all work; there were breaks. When the weather was bad, the boat couldn't go out. On days like that, Alph repaired nets, but that didn't take long. When he finished his job each day, Alph was free. He spent most of his free time in Uncle Simon's carpenter shop. In the winter and sometimes in the spring, Alph would sometimes spend as much as a week working with Simon.

Alph's most unlikeable job when he was younger was carrying water. He'd had to do that at least once every day, and sometimes several times a day if Mother was washing. Water had to be carried in buckets from the lake, all the way up the hill to the house. There were only six houses between home and the water, but it seemed a long, long way when your bucket was full. Grandmother had helped him when he was smaller. They would each grab one side of the bucket, and up the hill they would go.

One day, Alph noticed that little Ruth and her friends, Sarah and Martha, were carrying water. The girls were all about the same size but two years apart. Ruth was the youngest, Sarah, Timothy's little sister a year older, and Martha the cobbler's daughter, was yet another year older. The girls were laughing and having a good time, but he remembered those days and wondered if there wasn't an easier way to carry water.

Later that day he was down by the dock, and saw a wagon someone was using to haul fish. Alph decided the wagon was an ingenious tool. What if the girls had a wagon? One of them could carry as much water as three without a wagon, and it would be much easier.

Alph told Simon of his wagon idea, and Simon thought it would be a good project. He suggested Alph tell Grandfather, who might have some metal parts that would make the wagon stronger. Grandfather thought it was a good idea and said he could come up with a couple of axels and some fasteners to hold the bed together. The idea was good, but now for the actual work. Simon had no left-over-boards, so Alph was going to have to start from scratch. Behind the shop were some logs that had been stored up off of the ground to season and dry. Simon picked one he thought would work and asked Simon if it was planned for any work.

"No," Simon said, "You can use it for your wagon."

So, Alph selected some wedges and a maul and started splitting the log into slabs. The next thing was to take an adze and smooth the slabs into boards. After a while, his material began to take shape. He would have to make two boards for the bottom, cut to the right size for two water buckets, then one for each side, and one for each end. After they were sized, Alph cut them to length, and the only thing left was to assemble them, and the bed was finished. Now he had to make the wheels. The pieces would have to be smooth and flat so they could be glued together with their grain at ninety degrees to each other. This would help keep them from splitting when they hit bumps. The process sounded simple, but it took several days of pain staking work just to get the material ready for assembly. But, it was fun and Alph enjoyed it. Simon taught him well and Alph was a good carpenter. Pretty soon it was time to head to Grandfather's for the metal work.

The rainy spell lasted just the right length of time. Ten days of cold, rainy, windy weather before the boat could go out again, was just the right length of time to finish the wagon. There were two water buckets in the back room at home. Alph took the wagon home and tried the water buckets. The two of them just fit. The wagon could be pulled alongside the lake, and using a dipper made by Grandfather, the two water buckets could be filled in just a few minutes.

He presented it to the girls and they had so much fun with it that they volunteered to haul water for the neighbors.

Now, it was back to work on the fishing boat. Alph saw no challenge in fishing. There were small things to be mastered, little tricks to learn if you wanted to be a good fisherman, but it was no challenge for Alph. When he was sitting in the back of the boat he was always thinking of carpenter things to do, like hanging a door, or the fun he had building the wagon for Little Ruth and her friends. Alph was proud however of working with his father. He knew that someday it would be Simon and Son, Fishermen, and then eventually his business.

Isaac had been watching Alph for several months as they fished the Sea of Galilee. Alph worked hard and never complained. He always seemed to enjoy his work and carried as much of a load as any man.

It was almost Alph's fifteenth birthday. He rose from the dinner table one night at the same time as his father. Eva was startled as she realized Alph was not much shorter than his father. She looked at him quizzically, then took him by one ear and turned him around to where the light that was coming into the house shined on his face.

"What did I do?" Alph asked as Eva examined his face.

"You've started becoming a man," she said. "You're almost as tall as you're father, and what is this growing on your chin and upper lip?"

Isaac started laughing and said, "What is the matter Mother? Don't you want your baby boy to grow up?"

Alph blushed. He certainly didn't want to be the subject of a very personal family discussion about him, and so he hurried out the nearest door.

One evening Mother Ruth, Grandpa, Grandfather, Simon and Mary were all at Isaac and Eva's for dinner. It was no special occasion. They did it often and the family enjoyed being together. After dinner Little Ruth was out the door to find her friends, and Mother Ruth and Mary were helping Eva clean up after the meal. Grandpa, Grandfather, Simon and Isaac were all gathered on the benches outside. Isaac had asked Simon to build some extra benches and install them for the men's gathering place.

Isaac was chewing on a straw and suddenly asked Alph, "Son, if you could work at any trade you wanted, if there were no family ties, no tradition, what would that work be?"

Alph felt his face flush. He didn't want to lie to Papa, and he didn't want to lie to himself either. That too would be wrong. He thought for a long time and everyone was waiting for his answer, and then he gave a wise answer for a young man.

He said, "Papa, I could learn from Grandfather and be a metal smith, I could learn from Grandpa and become a potter, from Simon and be a carpenter or you and be a fisherman, but tradition says I should follow my father."

All was quiet for a while, and then the conversation went on to other subjects. Eva called little Ruth in for bed and Isaac told

Alph he should probably do the same, tomorrow would be a big day. Alph went in and got his bed mat and went up on the roof.

He heard Uncle Simon say, "Isaac, I have never told you anything about raising you children. You are a good father, but I want to offer this. Alph is the best natural carpenter I have ever met. I have seen carpenters who have been in business for years and years who aren't as talented as he is.

After that their voices dropped off and Alph could hear them talking but not what they were saying. Soon he dropped off to sleep.

In the morning Papa woke Alph for breakfast and said, "Alph, Fix yourself a lunch to take with you today. You won't be eating with me. You are to go to your Uncle Simon's and will be working with him from now on."

Alph wished he knew what had been said after he went to bed the night before, but he never found out and never again was anything ever said about Alph the fisherman, it was Alph the carpenter.

Alph's training as a carpenter became more intense. Simon taught him how to make a square corner with a three-by-four-by-five triangle, how to use a plumb bob, how to set a plumb line, how to find the center of a circle and much more.

Several months after Alph started working for Uncle Simon, and while they were alone, Isaac said to him, "Son. I have been told that you are a very good carpenter. I am proud of you." That was the last that was ever said of the matter, but Alph still wondered what was said that night after he went to bed.

11

AN EXCITING TRIP FOR
NEW TOOLS

One day Simon told Alph that there was a furniture shop in Tiberius that was going out of business. The owner had died, and his widow wanted to sell all of his tools. "I think we should harness Plato and go have a look," Simon said. "There may be some tools that would be nice to have in our shop."

They got everything ready and early the next morning they left for Tiberius.

When they found the shop, the man's widow was anxious to show them what she had. There was no one in Tiberius that was interested in the tools, and no one else had come to look. The shop had so many tools, that Alph didn't even know the name of some of them. There were many tools; draw knives, saws, planes, and metal hammers, as well as a lathe. Alph asked Simon what the lathe was for. Simon told him it was for making things round; legs, posts, dowels, and even wooden dishes. It took two men to run it. One supplied the power and the other did the cutting with gauges.

Simon told the woman that he wouldn't have the money to buy it all. If she would set some individual prices, he would buy what he could afford.

"She looked around the room and sighed. How much money do you have?" she asked.

When Simon told her, she said that she wanted to dispose of it all. If Simon would give her all the money he had, he could have everything. Simon was overwhelmed. The tools were worth far more than he could offer, but she said there was no one else interested, and she wanted them to go to someone who would use them and care for them. The deal was made and they started loading the cart.

It had taken all day to get to Tiberius, make the deal, and load Plato's cart. The cart was really full. Now the sun was setting. The woman told them they could spend the night in the shop, so they put their sleeping mats down and slept.

They left at first light. The road back to Capernaum ran along the Sea of Galilee and had very few hills. Thy held the cart or pushed it, whichever was needed to help Plato, but the cart was so heavy they stopped often to let him rest. They weren't far from home when one of the wheels hit a bump and broke. The right side of the cart went clear to the ground and left the whole thing leaning at a precarious angle. There wasn't any choice in what they had to do. Simon would have to unhook Plato from the cart, strap the broken wheel on his back, and take the wheel to their shop and repair it. Alph would have to stay with their new tools.

There were quite a few travelers on the road between Tiberius and Capernaum, and many of them stopped to see if they could help. Some stopped and took rest breaks and offer Alph food. Toward evening traffic slowed and as the sun was low it stopped all together. Alph hadn't worried during the afternoon when there were lots of people, but now he was getting nervous. It didn't help when he saw two rough looking men coming toward him.

They stopped and asked what he had in the cart. Alph told them carpenter tools. They didn't say anything else but untied the rope that held the load. They began laying things on the ground. Alph told them that his uncle and some friends were coming, but it didn't stop them. They just kept unloading the cart, thinking they would find something good. Alph didn't know whether to stay or run. He was pretty sure he could outrun them but thought he should stay to protect their valuables, although he didn't think he was doing a very good job of that.

Suddenly, they heard the sound of many people coming up the road, and around the bend came ten mounted Roman soldiers and a hundred foot soldiers marching behind them. The men looting the cart saw them coming and ran, but the centurion in charge sent two of the men on horseback after them, and they didn't get far. The robbers were told to sit on the grass beside the road, and the centurion told the soldiers to tie them up and check them for weapons.

The centurion dismounted and introduced himself, and asked Alph what had happened. After Alph told his story, the centurion told him they had been hunting these two robbers for a long time but could never catch them. He also told Alph not to worry. He would leave four men to stay with him till his uncle returned. Then he called his men back into formation, and they continued their march, taking the robbers with them.

After the troop of Roman soldiers left, the four that stayed set down and introduced themselves to Alph. They were about his age, and three of them were Greeks who had joined the Roman army to gain Roman citizenship. The fourth said his name was Atticus and he had been born in a village just out of Rome. He had joined the army for adventure. The men opened their packs and offered Alph some food. By now it was dark, and the soldiers gathered some firewood and started a fire.

Alph didn't think that Simon would come back during the night, but when Isaac heard of their problem, he realized that Alph was alone with the cart, and he was worried. There was a full moon for them to see by, so he, Simon, and Nikos came in the middle of the night. Everything was safe now, so they decided to get some sleep till morning. At first light the soldiers lifted the bad side of the cart while Simon and Isaac put the new wheel on. They repacked the cart and were ready to go in a short while.

One of the soldiers said if they were hungry, there was an inn just up the road where they had bought bread and wine the day before. Isaac said he would buy everyone breakfast if they would join them. So the men joined together for a meal before they went their separate ways. The inn keeper even had hay and grain for Plato.

They got home later that day, and everyone was so tired they just unhooked Plato from the cart and went to rest. Alph led Plato over to his pen, fed him, and rubbed him down while he talked to him.

They were back in Capernaum with a new adventure for the list of stories to be told.

12

AN ADULT BIRTHDAY

There was one thing that could be said for Eva and her men. No man in the community was any better dressed or groomed than Isaac or Alph. If either of them tore a piece of clothing, he had best not put it back on until it was checked and repaired by Eva. She had always cut and trimmed Isaac's hair and beard, and now with Alph growing facial hair, she had it to trim too. Alph probably had most of his growth. He was just a slight bit taller than his father and had inherited enough Greek genes that his hair and beard were curly, thick, and black as the coal tar used to calk houses. In addition this well groomed young man with thick, shortly trimmed beard and hair was handsome to look at and sported a shy smile permanently etched on his face. His personality made him pleasant to be around but nervous when the young women stared and giggled.

Today, because it was the day before the Sabbath, the women had spent most of their time in the kitchen, preparing their usual big family meal. The Sabbath began at sunset, and the family had just finished eating. Mother, Mary, Grandmother, and Little Ruth didn't need a special reason to cook. They liked cooking and all of the men liked eating, especially Grandfather and Grandpa, who were getting a little bit chunky. It had gotten to be a family practice to have the largest meal of the week just before the Sabbath started, but today was a special day. Today they were celebrating birthdays. Alph was eighteen and Little Ruth was thirteen, big days in their lives. Both would now be considered adults. After congratulatory remarks, Isaac asked if they felt any different. Ruth said she didn't feel any different but that from now on she would like to be called Ruth, not Little Ruth.

Before anyone else could comment, Grandmother Ruth spoke up. She said, "When Ruth was born, I was honored to have her named Ruth, but to distinguish us we agreed to call her Little Ruth. This was a good thing, but she is no longer Little Ruth. She is matured and is taller than I. She needs to be called by her own name. If you need to distinguish us, you can call me Mother Ruth, or grandmother. Either one will do. But, out of respect to Ruth she needs to be called by her right name, Ruth, not a name that indicates a copy of her grandmother.

Everyone agreed and took turns saying, "Hello Ruth."

Then Alph spoke up and said that he had always called his father Papa, but that was like a little boy. "I am going to start calling him Father." But then he smiled. "Sometimes I will call him Papa. Father sounds kind of stuffy." Everyone laughed.

Isaac laughed and asked if there were any more name changes in the family.

"Well," Simon said. "Yes there are. Soon, Mary and I hope to be called Mother and Papa."

It took a moment for what he had said to soak in. Isaac caught it first and said, "Congratulations to the new parents." Then everyone applauded.

It had been a grand evening. Tomorrow would be a day of rest before a new work week. Everyone was well fed. The men drifted off to the benches to talk for a while, about everything they didn't know anything about. The women put up what was necessary and left the rest until after the Sabbath. And Alph, who preferred sleeping on the roof under the stars disappeared as everyone else trickled off to their own beds.

13

THE MAN THEY CALL JESUS

When his eyes opened some of the night's stars had already disappeared. One by one and two by two, they were just starting to twinkle out, as the sky began to change in preparation for the coming of the morning sun. Alph scurried to his feet, rolled up his bed mat, and went down the stairs. On the table, lying beneath a cloth, were some uneaten crusts of Mother's bread. Although they were two days old, they were still soft and chewy. A good handful of them would make a good breakfast. Alph slipped quietly through the house; so as not to wake the family; and went down the street, munching on the tough, tasty crust as he walked toward the dock. There was still a while before the sun would break into sight. The last few stars held their places in the sky, and there was still enough of the moon's light to glisten on the ripples of the waters of Galilee.

A small group of men had assembled on the dock.

As Alph approached he could see the two brothers, Andrew and Simon, and three other fishermen he didn't know engaged in conversation. Andrew was doing the talking. He had been down by the Jordan listening to a man named John. He said his preaching was spellbinding and told what happened.

He said that John had said, "You brood of snakes! Who told you to flee God's coming anger? Don't just say to each other that you are safe because you are descendants of Abraham. Prove it by the way you live. Repent and turn to God. What you have done means nothing, I tell you. God can create children of Abraham from these very stones. The ax of God's judgment is poised, ready to sever the roots of the trees. Every tree that does not produce good fruit will be chopped down and thrown into the fire."

The crowd asked. "What should we do?"

And John replied, "If you have two shirts, give one to the poor. If you have food, share it with the hungry."

Even corrupt tax collectors came to be baptized and asked what they should do. John told them. "Collect no more than the government requires."

"What should we do," asked some soldiers.

"Don't extort money or make false accusations." John said. "Be content with your pay."

Everyone was expecting the Messiah to come soon, and they were eager to know if John might be the Messiah. John answered their questions by saying, "I baptize you with water; but someone is coming soon who is greater than I am. He is so much greater that I am not even worthy to be his slave and untie the straps of his sandals. He will baptize you with the Holy Spirit and with fire. He is ready to separate the chaff from the wheat with his winnowing fork and will clean up the threshing area, gathering the wheat into his barn and burning the chaff with never ending fire." John used many warnings as he announced the good news to the people.

Andrew continued. "I listened as he continued to preach. I believe him, and I think the Messiah is coming. I feel it. I know it's the truth."

None of the other men spoke, not even his brother, Simon.

Alph walked away to go to the carpenter shop and think about what Andrew had said. Alph worked all day in silence, saying nothing about it to his uncle Simon. A couple of times Simon asked him if he felt all right. It wasn't like Alph to not be chatty while he worked. Alph put him off by saying he was fine, he was just thinking of some things he had heard, so Simon dropped the subject.

As Alph worked, he asked himself, "What does this mean? Who is John? Andrew is an honest man, a devout Jew. He seems to believe in John. I need to talk to Papa."

After work, Alph looked down at the lake. The fishing boats were just coming in for the day. Papa's boat was already there and unloaded, so Alph walked down to the dock to meet Isaac as he headed toward home.

They started up the hill and as soon as they were out of earshot of the men at the dock, Alph said, "Father! This morning I woke early and walked down to the lake. Five men were there talking, and as I walked up, Andrew was telling about a man named John. Andrew said he was down on the Jordan, and John was baptizing people for the remission of their sins and proclaiming the coming of the Messiah. Andrew says that this John knows what he is talking about, that he is a prophet of God."

Isaac said, "I heard Andrew speaking of this last week. I think we should take off work and go down and see for ourselves."

Alph agreed, and when they got home, Isaac told Eva that he and Alph were going down on the Jordan across from Jericho next week, to hear a man named John who was preaching about the coming of the Messiah. Eva said she had just heard of him today. Mary had been talking to the wife of Simon, the fisherman, Andrew's brother. She said that Andrew is convinced that it is all true. The Messiah is coming! The kingdom of God is at hand!

This was pretty radical talk, so they all agreed that they wouldn't talk to anyone else about it until they had more facts. Isaac and Alph would leave to go down to the Jordan on the second day after the next Sabbath to hear John and witness his baptisms.

Alph told Simon what he and Isaac were going to do, and Simon replied that he too had heard of John's preaching. He said that he would like to go with them but he had an appointment, to talk to a man about some important work for the carpenter shop. In fact, he would be going out of town too. "We will just close the shop for a few days while we are all gone," Simon said. "When I get back I may have some important news to share with you. Wish me well, because if it works out, it will mean a lot to us."

Alph was so anxious to hear John it seemed like the day of he and Isaac's departure would never come. When it did, they were on the road early in the morning. The traffic was heavier than usual, and most of the talk on the road was about this profit named John. A group of men walked just ahead of Alph and Isaac. Their conversation was easy to hear.

There will be an anointed one.

"No, the anointed one was King David," argued the older man.

"But, there is another one to come. It will be he who will restore the throne of David. He is the one we await now."

They walked a little further, and then the younger man continued, "If David's throne is to be restored, there must be an army. Where will that Army come from?"

The old man said, "It will be as it was with Moses and Joshua and David. God will tell him what to do.

Isaac nudged Alph and picked up the pace so they could pass the men. As they passed, Isaac smiled at them and gave them a greeting. They continued on until they were a ways ahead of them before either of them spoke.

After they were well out of ear shot Alph said, "Father, how much of what they said do you think was true?"

Isaac said, "Well, I know that some of it was true, but I think much was misinformation received from gossip and guessing."

They continued their pace until mid-day. They were at a place where the river was not far from the road, so they stopped under a large tree along the bank and took some bread and cheese out of their packs, dipped some water from the stream, and sat down to rest and eat. After a short rest they got up and continued their walk. If they stayed at a good pace they could probably make it to Jericho in four days or five at the most.

As they walked they talked about what they saw and what the family might be doing. They also wondered what Simon was working on.

The next day as they were walking, Isaac looked at Alph, "Your mother and I have been wondering if you have taken a liking to any of the girls you know. You are at marrying age, but have shown no prospects. We have wondered if maybe we should find a match-maker for you and make some arrangements."

The subject didn't seem to embarrass Alph. He simply said, "No, I would rather find my own wife as you and Mother did. I will let you know when I find someone. There is time. I am not ancient.

Isaac just laughed, patted Alph on the back, and said. "Okay." And the subject was dropped.

Just before evening of the fourth day, they saw a crowd gathered along the river not far from Jericho. As they approached, the crowd began to scatter. Isaac asked a group of them if this was where John was preaching. They said, "Yes, but he is finished for the day and is going off into the wilderness. This is the way he does in the evenings, but he will return in the morning, or at least it is the way he has done."

So, Isaac and Alph found a smooth, comfortable place for the night along the Jordan.

The next morning John showed up at the Jordan again and started preaching and baptizing. Alph had lain awake during part of the night thinking, "I don't think I am a sinner. I am a Jew and have always followed my father's teaching. I have been to school and studied the law and have done my very best to observe it. Why do I need to be forgiven? What have I done wrong? But still

95

Alph felt something missing. He decided that in the morning, he would go down into the water and be baptized by John.

So, the next morning, when John went down into the water, Alph started toward him. As he reached John, he realized that Isaac had walked down with him. So, together they were baptized by John and walked together, arm in arm, father and son, back to their place on the bank.

After John had preached for a while longer, a man walked down into the river. The man was Jesus, and he asked John to baptize him, but John said, "No. I need to be baptized by you. Why do you come to me?

Jesus answered him saying, "Let it be so. It's proper for us to do this to fulfill all righteousness."

Then John consented and baptized Jesus.

After Jesus was baptized, he was coming up out of the water, and the heavens opened up and the spirit of God, looking like a dove, lighted on him.

Then a voice out of the Heavens said, "THIS IS MY SON, THE BELOVED, WITH WHOM I AM WELL PLEASED."

Alph and Isaac saw the dove and heard the voice, and they felt safe, warm, and comforted, like they had never felt before. The voice had come from everywhere and was soft and gentle, not loud, yet dominated all other sounds. No one spoke, the birds quit singing, the water in the river flowed without a sound, and the crowd was in awe. Not one person was moving. Then, slowly they began moving up and out of the river.

Isaac and Alph stayed and listened to John for two more days before they headed home. Until now they had not discussed what they had seen and heard.

Even now, they traveled some distance before either said a word. Isaac was first to speak. He said, "Son, I think we have heard the voice of God and witnessed the coming of the Messiah."

Then he and Alph continued to walk in silence. Neither one of them knew what else to say. Finally, their conversation returned to normal and they made small talk the rest of the way home.

When they reached home the entire family was waiting to hear what Isaac and Alph had seen and heard. Everyone hung onto every word they said. Eva finally asked, "Do you think this man Jesus can really be the Messiah?"

"I want to see and hear more of what he has to say," Said Isaac, "But I think he is?"

14

THE PARTY

The next day, Timothy came over to see Alph and asked if the woodshop was going to be closed a few more days. Alph said that it would be closed until Simon returned from his trip.

"Well then," said Timothy. "There is a wedding at Cana the day after tomorrow. Several men we went to school with are going to be there. Let's go visit, see the girls, and enjoy the festivities."

Alph laughed and said, "That might be a good trip. We could leave early in the morning."

At first light they were on their way. They laughed and talked the whole day. They didn't get a chance to visit much anymore, since Alph was working in the Woodshop every day, and they had a lot of catching up to do on what the other was doing. They found a good camping spot in the evening, slept late the next day and arrived in the midmorning.

Timothy found them an empty table at the feast, and they sat down and looked over the crowd. It was larger than they thought it would be. Alph spotted the groom and several other young men that he and Timothy had gone to school with. Across the room from them was a table of girls that were laughing and having a really good time. Alph spotted one of them that was just about the prettiest girl he had ever seen. He couldn't quit looking at her. In a few minutes he noticed that when he would look at her, she would turn her head and look away from him. If he kept looking, she would turn and look back at him and the both of them would quickly turn away. He tried to watch her out of the corner of his eye but it was unsuccessful. Finally he asked Timothy if he knew who she was.

Timothy said, "Do you mean that girl you have been playing eyes with?

"Was I that obvious," he said.

Timothy kept laughing at him and said, "Yes, that's the one I thought. Both of you are having trouble trying to stare at the other without getting caught. Alph! She is your little sister's friend, Martha, the cobbler's daughter. She and Ruth played together when they were little girls. She must have been over at your house several days a week for years."

Alph couldn't believe it. She is grown up, and beautiful along with it.

"Believe it," said Timothy. "She is two years older than Ruth, and if you haven't noticed yet, your little sister is grown up and beautiful too. Little girls grow up."

Alph thought it best to look around and see who else was there that he knew. Just then Jesus came in with his disciples and an older woman who must be his mother. They took seats at a large table to their left.

Timothy and Alph hadn't yet gotten any wine, so Alph asked a waiter if they could get some. The waiter said they were out, but that the headwaiter was going to get some.

He wasn't trying to eavesdrop, but he couldn't help but hear the conversation at Jesus' table. His mother told him they were out of wine, but Jesus asked her what that had to do with him. He said, "You know I haven't yet come into my time."

Alph didn't know what he meant, but noticed that his mother ignored him and told a waiter that they were to do whatever he told them.

Jesus looked like he wasn't too happy with his mother, but he told the waiter they were to fill the large urns along the wall with water. In a few minutes there was a hush-hush conversation between the waiter and the headwaiter. After they moved on off he noticed the waiters dipping the water they had put in the urns, tasting it, and then looking surprised.

Alph waited until everything settled down. Timothy had been busy visiting friends. So, he took their cups over and dipped them into the urns. When Timothy came back to the table he took a sip out of his cup and said, "When did they serve this wine? It's the best I've ever tasted."

Alph told him to wait until they were on the way home and he would tell him a story about it.

When afternoon came they decided they had better start on their way soon. If they did, they could be home by tomorrow evening.

When they stood up to leave, Jesus and Alph stood up at the same time, and looked directly into each other's eyes. Alph felt like he had never had anyone look at him like that before. He knew that Jesus was looking into his soul. He knew what Alph was thinking, who he was, and what kind of person he was. He wondered if he had Jesus' approval. It only lasted a few seconds and then Jesus gave him a smile and they moved on. As they started their journey Alph felt stunned. He felt like he had been inspected by the Messiah.

As they walked down the road toward Capernaum, Alph told Timothy how the wine in the urns came to be. Timothy said nothing but Alph could tell by the look on his face that Timothy was having a hard time believing it, so he dropped the matter.

15

PASSOVER AND ROMANCE

It was time for Passover, and many of their friends were going to Jerusalem. Mother Ruth and Grandpa had never been there, and several neighbors had children who had never been to Jerusalem. So, the family and their neighbors decided to travel to Jerusalem together this year. They packed up the things they'd need, and even made a place in Plato's cart, along with their food, for one or two small children to ride when they got tired. Grandmother Ruth decided she would go next time. It was too close to the time for the coming of Mary's child, and she would stay with Mary and Simon.

Grandpa and Grandfather would take the lead, walking ahead with Plato and the cart. Alph, Ruth, Martha and Timothy would walk behind them with the children, which made Alph a little nervous. He hadn't spoken to Martha since the party at Cana.

Isaac, Eva, Abe and Rebeca along with Timothy's parents, younger sister and other neighbors would follow. In all it would be twenty to thirty people and a long seven to eight day trip. If they left at a time so as to put the Sabbath in the middle, it would give them a day's rest about half way.

This caravan of pilgrims from Capernaum left early of a morning, starting down along the Sea of Galilee. Many of them had not slept well out of anticipation for the trip, so their energy level was low, even though they were excited. The children ran back and forth all morning, making their journey twice as far, but by noon they were worn down to a quiet walk. By evening both Alph and Timothy were carrying tired children and were ready to stop. Alph stretched out on his bed-roll thinking how far they had yet to go.

The next morning as they started again, Timothy thought some games might occupy the children. They were in a rugged area and he told the children they might catch sight of some conies playing in the rocks. Pretty soon the children were watching to see who would be the first to see a Coney. Then to see who could count the most conies, and Alph tried to get them to see who could get the closest to one of them, before it ran away. The Conies were as afraid of the children as much as the children were of the Conies.

In the morning light, they could still see the Sea of Galilee, but were starting down into the Jordan River Valley. The road curved right, then left and then down, down, down as it descended into the valley by a series of little hills. The group had stretched out a bit and once when they came around a little curve, Alph saw Ruth and Timothy walking side by side and holding hands. They probably thought they couldn't be seen. They had grown up together like brother and sister, but Alph thought to himself that this relationship was not brother and sister. He was wondering if he was now seeing his sister Ruth and his future brother-in-law. It would keep for now but later he would find time to let them know what he had seen. Hmmm. My best friend, my brother-in-law. Alph grinned.

Later, Alph and Martha were walking side by side watching the children ahead of them when impulse took over and Alph took ahold of Martha's hand. For a moment he wondered what he would do if she pulled away, but she just looked up at him and smiled and gave his hand a little squeeze. After that, they spent a good bit of time walking together, hand in hand. Once they caught up with Ruth and Timothy. Ruth looked startled when she saw them and dropped Timothy's hand. Then they saw Alph and Martha holding hands, and they all started laughing.

Martha had a timbrel and sometimes would take it out of her pack and start singing hymns as she beat on it. The children would learn the song quickly and by the end of the day sounded like a Junior Temple Choir.

The Sabbath came and everyone was at rest, some were sleeping; maybe some were daydreaming, and others were sitting and talking. Alph, Martha, Timothy and Ruth gathered their charges together in a circle, trying to keep the children as quiet as they could, which was a big job. Alph began telling the story of Isaac's trip to Egypt. Then he told the story of the broken wheel, when the robbers tried to steal the cartload of carpenter tools, while Simon was gone. He told them why his father walked with a limp, and it seemed his stories could go on forever and the children could listen forever. Alph loved to tell stories and adults as well as children loved to listen.

The next day was the first day of the week, everyone was rested, the air was fresh, the morning dew made the grass and leaves sparkle, and everyone was still clean and fresh from having cleaned up for the Sabbath. Alph and Martha were walking along together when Alph said, "I have a confession to make. When we were at the wedding feast in Cana, I saw you across the room and didn't recognize you. I thought you were the prettiest girl I had ever seen. I was sneaking looks and turning away when I thought you were looking. When Timothy told me who you were, I couldn't believe it. I had always thought of you as Ruth's little friend, and I had been so caught up in my work and hadn't seen you for a long time. It was a very pleasant surprise. I'm glad I went, and I'm glad we're on this trip together.

"Will you not laugh if I tell you something?" Martha said.

"Of course not," said Alph.

When Ruth and I were about twelve and fourteen, I used to tell her that someday I was going to marry someone like her brother, and she always laughed at me and told me I was silly, but I thought you were the nicest and most handsome man I had ever seen." She giggled. "Also, I saw you sneaking looks at me in Cana, and I liked it." And don't tell me you didn't notice all the girls there were watching you and giggling. I could turn away and they would tell me if you were looking at me."

Just then two of the children got into an argument and they had to shift their attention.

They were near Jericho. Isaac said it would be best to stop now for the evening and get a good rest before starting up the mountain in the morning. Then they would be starting fresh with a lot more energy. When morning came, it was cloudy and cool but didn't look like rain. That would be ideal for keeping the group from overheating. A group would have to follow the donkey cart and take turns pushing on it to help Plato. It wasn't loaded as heavy as some of their past trips but it was a long way up the mountain. After a long day of pushing and climbing they broke over a rise in the road and could see the city of David with its walls and gates and the temple. People were camped everywhere.

There was no hope of finding a camping spot inside the walls, so they pulled off of the road, while Isaac, Alph and Timothy went to find a place to set up their camp. Walking toward the Damascus gate they saw a place not yet occupied that looked like there was room for them, so Isaac stayed there to guard it while Alph and Timothy went back and brought up the little caravan from Capernaum. They set up tents and made limits for where the children could go without an adult.

Their food rations were running low, so Eva, Ruth, and Martha, with Alph and Timothy as their security guards went to find a market and re-stock their supplies. The choices were plentiful, but prices were higher than what they were used to in

Capernaum. By dark they were settled down and had met several of their camping neighbors. They met people from all over Galilee and Judea.

When Isaac and Eva settled down for the night, Isaac laid thinking about his teenage years when he had come to Jerusalem by himself. A lot had happened since those days. At sixteen he had been free to roam, but he believed he preferred today. He had been to Jerusalem several times since those days, and each time had wondered about his old friend Edfu. Was he still alive? Did he ever come back to Jerusalem again with a caravan? Every time he saw a caravan, he looked at the camel drivers but wasn't sure he'd recognize Edfu if he did see him.

The next morning Grandpa and Grandfather elected to stay and watch the camp while the rest went sightseeing. They broke into three groups so it would be easier to keep everyone accounted for, and toured the city and the temple. The young ones were fascinated by all of the people, the shops, and the temple. When they got tired they headed back to camp to rest. Sightseeing was more work than walking the road on the trip.

A report of Jesus' healings spread through the camps around Jerusalem. Everyone wondered who he was. Many, including Isaac and Alph were sure he was the Messiah, the son of God. The next day Alph and Timothy took a walk to the temple. Alph wanted to hear his words and maybe get a chance to see some of his miracles. They had no more than gotten there when they heard a commotion and a lot of yelling. They followed the noise and saw Jesus with a homemade whip. He was scattering the animals and upsetting the tables of the money changers. Men were screaming and calling him names but he paid no attention to them until he got everything upset, Then he took his whip, chased the animals, including the cattle and the sheep, along with the men that were doing business in the temple. He was shouting at them, "Get these things out of here! My father's house is not a place for you to do business."

Some of the Jewish leaders were there and they shouted back at him, "By what authority are you doing these things? What sign will you show us?"

Then Jesus answered them saying, "Destroy this temple and in three days I will raise it back up!"

The leaders replied, "It took forty-six years to build this temple, and you're going to raise it up in three days?"

Then Jesus walked off into the crowd, and no one knew where he went.

Alph and Timothy walked back to the camp and on the way Timothy turned to Alph and said, "I was skeptical when you first told me about Jesus, but now I believe you. He is the son of God." When they got to camp, they found Isaac, and told him everything they had seen and heard.

"Come with me," Isaac said, and took Eva by the hand. "I want to go up to the temple and see what is happening."

They walked around the temple for a while, and then Isaac saw Jesus talking to some people over on some steps. When they got there Jesus was teaching them, and saying, "For God so loved the world that he gave his only son, so that everyone who believes in him won't parish, but have eternal life. God didn't send his son into the world to judge the world, but that the world might be saved through him."

They walked back to camp talking about what Jesus had said. When they got there, Isaac told everyone what they had seen and heard.

One evening Isaac told Eva he was going for a walk.

"You're going to look for Edfu aren't you?" she said.

"Yes, but it's doubtful I will find him, or ever see him again. For all I know, he may be dead."

So, he started out alone, walking around the city, looking for a camel caravan. He found two, and asked some of the drivers if they had seen a very tall Egyptian man named Edfu. One man said that he had worked with him a couple of years ago but hadn't seen him in quite a while. That was some encouragement, so Isaac kept walking and looking for camel drivers. It was dark and beginning to get late. He knew that Eva would be worried so he turned toward the direction of their camp. Then he saw a group of camel drivers around a camp-fire and heard a distinctive voice, one that he would never forget. "EDFU!" Isaac shouted loudly, and the man turned around.

"Is that my young friend Alph?"

The two men embraced as long, lost brothers. Edfu had some gray in his hair, but had changed very little otherwise. Isaac, on the other hand, had grown and was heavier, but Edfu still recognized him.

"Can you get away for a little while?" Isaac said. "I have some people I want you to meet.

"Yes," Said Edfu. "We don't leave for two more days. I will get a friend to see after my camel."

The two men walked toward Isaac's camp, talking the whole way, unable to get everything in. When they got there Isaac found Eva and said, "Eva, this is my friend Edfu. We traveled back from Egypt together."

"So this is my young brother Alph and his wife." Edfu said; "My little brother, who saved my life and fed me until I was well, you know"

Everyone looked at Edfu a little strangely until Isaac said, "No one knows me by that name, Edfu. I am known as Isaac, and this man is Alf, my son, named after our experience together, and this young woman is our daughter Ruth."

After everyone was introduced, they sat around the camp-fire drinking wine and telling stories, until everyone was falling asleep. Isaac found something to make a sleeping mat for Edfu and they settled down for the night,

The next day held more storytelling, eating, drinking wine and enjoying the day. In the evening, Edfu said he had to get back to his camp, so he excused himself, and Isaac walked part way with him. Isaac extended Edfu an invitation to come to Capernaum and Edfu told him that he just may do that one day. And once again, the two friends parted.

The children and even some of the adults were starting to get homesick. It was decided they would leave at the first sign of light in the morning. They got everything packed up so that in the morning they could just eat; pick up their beds, and leave.

It was cloudy, there was no moon in the sky, and Alph had just gotten to sleep when the first big boom sounded. Someone rebuilt the camp fire, and everyone got busy preparing their beds and tents for rain. Thunder was getting closer and more frequent. Alph's little tent was one he had made for himself just for the trip. It was made of lamb-skin and cozy just for one. After the first boom he had gotten company in the form of a little six-year-old girl, with a new arrival after almost every boom. Before long every small child in camp was piled into Alph's tent, sleeping on one-another, with Alph curled up in the doorway trying to get comfortable, and wondering what to do when the rain started. It was nice to be loved, trusted, and looked up to by all of these children, but this was more than he really needed. Fortunately the booms became softer, less frequent and the first drop of rain never fell. After all had gotten quiet, Alph looked up and could see stars. He pulled his bed mat out, laid it crossways in front of the tent, and tied the tent flap back. The children were in a pile inside the tent when their parents came to collect them in the morning for breakfast.

As soon as they were finished, they harnessed Plato and started down the mountain. Going down was much easier than it had been coming up. The children were instructed that they could hold on to the back of the cart and slide their feet to keep the cart from pushing so hard on Plato. Grandfather and Grandpa had to watch or there would be so many holding on that Plato had to pull the cart going down-hill. They were more than halfway down when Grandpa said there was a flat area where they could pull over for lunch.

Isaac, Alph, and Timothy walked over to where they could see on down the mountain. They figured that they could be down to a flat spot near the bottom by evening, where they could camp for the night. By the time the sun was behind the mountain they had reached the flat spot they had seen from above and pulled in for camping.

After dinner the light began to fade, they were sitting around the camp fire, talking about home and the time they had spent in Jerusalem. Alph and Martha, and Timothy and Ruth were sitting on some rocks near the back, holding hands down low where they wouldn't be seen. The children started laughing and pointed to them, saying, "Look at the love birds holding hands." Hands fell away as if they had been holding hot rocks. Isaac jumped to his feet, grabbed Eva by the hand and pulled her up. He started singing and skipping around the fire, swinging his and Eva's hands. Everyone started laughing, even the four red-faced young people. It had been obvious for many days that romance was in the air.

Each day was like the last as they traveled up the valley toward Galilee. Grandfather and Grandpa walked along, one on each side of Plato, talking about the days of their youth, their families, and their beloved members who had gone on to be with their ancestors. The young people, Alph, Martha, Timothy, and Ruth followed along with the children. Sometimes it looked as if they were all children as they played, talked, and sang. The rest of the adults just walked along behind, talking and just passing the time.

The day before the Sabbath, Alph noticed that the adults had fallen back, just enough to be out of earshot. He took Martha's hand and slowed her down just enough to be out of the children's earshot. When he knew no one was paying any attention to them, he said, "Martha, I love you and would like to ask your father for your hand in marriage. How would you feel about that?"

Martha looked up and smiled and said, "I love you too, and I thought you would never ask."

Alph looked forward, then back, and then thought better of doing anything impetuous. So he just squeezed her hand and said,

"Now all I have to do is convince your father that I would be an ideal son-in-law, and then get our parents together to agree it's a wonderful thing."

"I know my father, Martha said." And believe me you have no problem with them, and I know you won't with your parents either. Just don't tell them you love me. Tell them we love each other."

With all that said, they walked on quietly sharing a wonderful secret.

At day's end they found a better place than usual to stop for the night. Tomorrow would be the Sabbath. Not only would it be their third Sabbath since leaving home, it would also be Passover, with a good place to rest, and room for the children some quiet activities.

The next morning the young adults had all the children together and Martha was leading them in some hymns for Passover. Alph was off to one side, and when Martha had finished with the children he made a motion to her that he was leaving. Then he started looking for his parents. He was in luck. They were sitting by themselves. Isaac was on his back, propped up on his elbows, chewing on a stem of grass as he was prone to do. Eva was sitting on an old log as they laughed and talked. Alph sat by his mother, but spoke to his father.

"Father, on our trip to hear John, you asked if I had any particular girl in mind for a wife. I told you no, because at the time I didn't. But, now I do. Martha and I love one another and want to be married. We would very much like our parents blessing.

"Eva spoke up and said, "Alph, your sweetheart is a kind, beautiful girl. I have known her since she was a child, have worked with her in the kitchen, and have seen what a good, moral, hard working girl she is. You could do no better if you searched all of Judah.

Then Isaac said "In matters such as this it is always best to listen to the woman. It is done and you have our blessing. Your mother and I, and probably everyone else in camp have been wondering about you two. What does Abe say?"

Alph said, "Martha says he will be okay with it, but what I would like, would be for a blessing from all four parents. I was thinking of going over to see Abe now."

"Why don't we go with Jewish tradition, son? Let me go over and talk to Abe. I will tell him he can make the announcement to everyone after dinner. I will wave my arm to you when it's all set."

Alph gave Isaac and Eva a hug and went back to Martha. He sat next to her and said, "Papa is going to see your father and will give me a signal if all is well, and he is going to suggest to your father that he make the announcement after dinner. I know it is going well, but I am terribly nervous right now."

Martha looked up at him, took hold of his arm, and put her head on his shoulder.

Alph could see Isaac when he reached Abe, but of course could hear nothing of their conversation.

When Isaac reached Abe he gave him his most pleasant smile and said to him, "Abe, might we have a talk about our children?"

Abe returned the smile and said, "Isaac, if it is about a blessing for them, I would be glad to hear what you have to say. Everyone in camp is talking about what a fine pair they make, and we agree. If we looked forever we would not find a finer young man for a son-in-law. If it is agreeable to you and Eva we are ready to give them our blessing.

Then Isaac took Abe's arm and said, "Then there is no disagreement. We think they are made for each other. Would you like to announce it after dinner?"

"I would be proud to make the announcement," Abe said.

Isaac said, "Fine." And he patted Abe on the back, as he walked off toward Eva.

When Isaac reached Eva he said, "It is done. Abe will make the announcement after dinner. Right now those two young people are waiting for me to raise my arm like this," and he gave Alph a big wave.

When Alph saw the wave, he jumped to his feet, grabbed Martha, and took hold of her as he had seen his father do with his mother, and swung her in a circle. Suddenly he stopped and put his fingers to his lips and said, "Don't any of you say anything until Martha's father announces after dinner that we are getting married. This is our secret for right now.

Children love secrets that they can keep from adults and they all swore they wouldn't say a word. Then one of the girls noticed Martha crying and said, "What's the matter Martha don't you want to marry Alph?

"Oh yes," she said. I'm crying because I'm happy.

At that point Alph gave her a big hug, which turned into a group hug, with everyone laughing. No one in the main group paid any attention, because by now they were getting use to the kids' antics.

Dinner time came but Martha and Alph couldn't eat. They just picked at their food, too nervous to eat. The children kept looking at each other and giggling. Finally, Abe stood up and called for everyone's attention.

He said, "This is a great day in the lives of two families, for they are going to be united in marriage. We have given our blessing to our daughter, Martha, and our future son-in-law, Alph, as they plan to be united as one. Wedding plans have not yet been made but will be announced after we return to Capernaum." Cheers went up so quickly that Abe could not say anything more, and people swarmed over Alph and Martha with congratulations.

Latter in the evening, after the camp settled down for the night, and Isaac and Eva lay in bed, Eva said, "Now what are we going to do about Ruth?"

"You mean Ruth and Timothy?"

"Yes." Eva said. "She is still too young. She needs to be at least a year or two older before we let her get married."

"I know." Isaac said. "I will think about it and do something when the time comes."

The last two days of the journey were easy. Everyone was ready for home and gaining energy the closer they got. They started up out of the Jordan valley and then shouts went out from the children when they saw the Sea of Galilee. The steep little grades were easy for Plato because everyone wanted to help push on his cart. It was mid-afternoon when the group of pilgrims reached home. Isaac volunteered to put Plato in his pen and feed him. The women rushed to see if Mary's baby had yet arrived and the children were running everywhere.

Mother Ruth met everyone as they came in and said the baby has not yet come but it wouldn't be long. Within a short time everyone had eaten and was on their bed or preparing to get there. It had been a good trip but it was good to be home.

16

JOY, SORROW, AND JOY

Joy, sadness, fear, humor, love, and good fortune all seemed to bundled up and then turned loose the month that followed their Jerusalem trip.

On their first day back in the wood-shop, Simon told Alph to have a seat. He said, "I have some things to tell you. First, there is no longer a reason to call you my apprentice. There is nothing more I can teach you. You can do anything in the shop as well as I. As my gift to you, my nephew, friend and former student, I am giving you a partnership in the business. Here after, it will be Simon and Alph's woodworking business."

"I don't know what to say," Alph marveled.

Simon went on, "You needn't say anything. Much of the money I have saved to expand has come from your work, and you are the closest thing I will ever have to a brother. Now this is the good part. I have been negotiating with the Romans to rebuild and repair their chariots. If one breaks down here in Galilee, they have to load it on a wagon and haul it to Jerusalem for repairs. I have also included Daniel. He will supply all the metal parts for repair.

And, I have thought of expanding into building construction and remodeling. We could hire a mason and a couple of apprentices and build residences and commercial buildings. We can't do all of this at once but it is certainly something to think about. First, we have to honor the contract on Roman chariots.

This was an exciting thing to go home and tell Martha and his parents.

Alph remembered the cradle that Simon had made for him and Ruth. It has been stored in Mother's pantry room since Ruth had outgrown it. He started digging and found it under several other items that had also been stored since who knows when. It was dirty but still in good shape. One of the stiles in the side was broken and one rocker had a crack, bet other than that, it was still in good condition. He found a place in the back of the carpenter shop where he could hide it and Simon would probably not notice it. When he was alone in the shop he worked on it, and it didn't take long to get it cleaned up, repaired, and looking like new. As soon as it was finished he took it home and told Ruth that when the baby came, she had the honor of presenting it to Simon and Mary.

It didn't take long. The next morning Simon went to get the midwife, and everyone knew that the baby was on its way. Isaac, both grandfathers and Alph took their waiting positions outside to support Simon. He was concerned because Mary was a little older than most mothers when they have their first child, but Grandpa assured him that many women had babies in their thirties and forties. Just because it was her first didn't mean that she would have trouble. In fact, you may have many more children yet.

"I know," said Simon, "but that doesn't mean I can't worry."

Mary and I have decided that if it's a boy we will name him John. We have no special reason except that it is a good strong Jewish name.

Everyone agreed it was a good choice, and with no other Johns, there would be no confusion as to who he was.

Ruth came out to where the men were waiting while Simon was still talking. She laughed and said, "Well, you don't have to worry about a girl's name because John is here and the father is invited in to meet him."

The rejoicing was short lived. Mother Ruth fell ill that night with severe chest pains and within three days was gone. She called for Isaac and Eva shortly before she died and said, "The pain in my chest is growing stronger, and soon I will be going to my ancestors. Everything I have is yours, Isaac. You are my son, I love you, and everything I have is yours." With those words she closed her eyes and went to sleep. By evening she had quit breathing and was gone to be with her ancestors. She was the oldest member of the family and had lived seventy eight years. Now there was only one Ruth.

The only joy in the family during the next few days was little John. Ruth brought the cradle in at their first family meal and said, "This cradle was made for Alph, passed down to me, and now Alph has cleaned and repaired it and it's ready for John.

Simon looked at it with a smile on his face and said, "I had forgotten this. It looks as good as the day I finished it. Thank you, Alph. We will have to see how many generations it will last.

The next day, people on the street were talking in little groups. When Isaac got to work, his men and some others told him that Jesus was selecting his apostles to go about with him. They said he had already chosen some of the fishermen in Capernaum. They said he had picked four from the crews that worked this dock. They were the two sets of brothers, Simon and Andrew, and James and John. That will put a load on the other Capernaum fishermen to keep up the fish supply. Right after the wedding in Cana, Jesus had moved to Capernaum and had spent much of his time teaching and healing in the area. Simon seemed to be one of his favorite followers. Jesus had healed his mother-in-law, when it looked like she was on her deathbed.

It wasn't long after this, that Alph was looking out of the shop door while he was working, and noticed Jesus walking up from the sea toward the mountain. A number of people were following him and Alph could see Isaac coming toward him. He went out to meet him and Isaac said to him, "Jesus has been teaching and preaching some powerful sermons, and I am going to follow him and hear what he has to say. I will get your mother and whoever is at the house and you get Simon and whoever he can contact and we will meet on the mountain."

When Alph got there he could see the rest of his family coming up, and waved at them. Jesus' apostles were gathered around him and he started teaching them. Alph found a seat where he could easily hear and the rest sat down around him.

When Jesus began to talk, it seemed as if he was talking directly to Alph, and that he should take to heart the things he was saying.

He said, "Happy are people who are hopeless, because the kingdom of heaven is theirs. Happy are people who grieve, because they will be made glad. Happy are people who are humble, because they will inherit the earth. Happy are people who are hungry and thirsty for righteousness, because they will be fed until they are full. Happy are people who show mercy, because they will receive mercy. Happy are people who have pure hearts, because they will see God. Happy are people who make peace, because they will be called God's children. Happy are people whose lives are harassed because they are righteous, because the kingdom of heaven is theirs. Happy are you when people insult you and harass you and speak all kinds of bad and false things about you, all because of me. Be full of joy and be glad, because you have a great reward in heaven. In the same way, people harassed the prophets who came before you."

Jesus continued to talk for a long time. He talked about murder, anger, and even name calling. He said that people should make things right with those who have something against them. Wives and husbands should be faithful to one another. Don't get divorced, be honest in all your dealings, don't be easily offended, love and help your neighbors, and when you give, do it anonymously, and don't be showy.

Jesus taught everyone how to pray. He said, "Pray like this. Say, "Our father who is in Heaven, holy is your name. May your kingdom come, and your will be done, here on earth as it is in heaven. Give us the bread we need today and forgive us our wrongs just as we forgive those who wrong us. Don't lead us into temptation but deliver us from evil; Amen."

He taught a lot more things, and all of the people were amazed, because his teaching was done with authority. After this he went on to heal the sick and lame, and Isaac and Alph led the family home. At the evening meal they discussed what Jesus had said, and no one could find any fault in anything he had taught. Everyone said, "I believe that Jesus is the Christ."

Alph said, "I think Jesus knows how we feel. I know that he looked into my heart and that he knows what I believe."

17

EMBARRASSMENT AND A WEDDING

It was warm and windy, and the wind was making the lake a little rough. Isaac and David decided it would best be a day of rest. They told their men to go home and spend the day with their families.

Isaac was sitting in front of the house, daydreaming when he saw a familiar face coming up the road. It was Benjamin, a man he knew from childhood but whom he hadn't seen in quite some time. Benjamin beamed when he saw Isaac and introduced the young woman with him as his daughter. She appeared to be about the same age as Ruth. Isaac called Ruth and introduced her to Esther saying, "Ruth, why don't you show Esther around and keep her company while her father and I get reacquainted and visit awhile?"

So, Ruth and Esther walked off, laughing and talking. Quite some time passed and Benjamin said, "Isaac, I need to leave before long. We have about a day and a half more of travel before we get home, and if we wait too long to leave we will have two nights on the road."

Just then Alph came in from work, and Isaac said, "This is Benjamin, an old friend. He and his daughter need to leave and Ruth has taken her walking somewhere. Would you see if you could find the girls so Esther and her father can get on the road?"

Alph agreed and started walking down the street toward the fish market. He passed a few people and asked if they had seen the two girls walking that way. No one had until he got to the fish market. The owner said they had walked over to the river and started up-stream, but he didn't see them again and had gone on about his work. So, Alph started up the river and walked for a pretty good distance. He had about decided to turn back, when he heard the girls laughing. He was just one little hill from the old swimming hole where Isaac and David used to swim, and where Isaac had taught him. As he topped the hill there was a sight. The girls had taken off their clothes, put them on bushes, and were having a water fight. The sight struck Alph funny, and he started laughing. The girls turned and saw him. Esther ducked down in the water until nothing was exposed but her face and the top of her head. Ruth was embarrassed but her reaction was to reach down to the bottom, grab a handful of mud, and throw it at Alph as she yelled, "Alph! I hate you!"

The mud ball broke apart before it reached him and splattered all over the ground in front of him, which tickled him more and he bent over laughing at her.

He turned his back to them, and as soon as he could regain his composure told them they needed to get dressed and come home, Benjamin wanted to get on the road.

Alph started walking back, and as soon as he was out of sight, the girls got out of the water and hurriedly got dressed in silence.

As they started walking, Esther said, "He won't tell will he?"

"He'd better not," said Ruth, and started running. "I know some secrets on him."

They caught up with Alph just a little way down the path. Esther was red-faced with her head hanging down.

Ruth caught Alph's arm, stopped him, and said, "Alph, you aren't going to tell Papa and Mother what we were doing, are you?" She looked up at this tall good looking man with thick, curly black hair and beard and realized they weren't children any more.

Alph looked down into her pleading eyes and said, "Ruth, when you were small, Mother used to have me bathe and dress you, tuck you into bed with a story, and kiss you good-night. As you grew up, I never told any of your tricks on you. Why should I begin now? You are my little sister, and I still love you."

Ruth pulled Alph down close to her and kissed him on his beard and said, "I told Esther you wouldn't tell because I knew some things on you, but I don't. You never do anything wrong, and if you did, Papa wouldn't do anything to you." Then, as an afterthought, she asked, "You aren't going to tell Timothy either, are you?"

Alph looked at her with his usual smile and said, "No. But you will someday and we will all laugh about it."

Esther was still greatly embarrassed, and kept looking down without saying a word.

When they got home, Eva asked where Alph had found them and he spoke up before the girls could answer, and said. "They were wading in the river." But, he didn't say what they were doing or how deep the water was.

Eva told Ruth to get some food for Esther and Benjamin to take with them, so they could eat on the road. Then she asked, "How did you girls get so wet. You look like you were swimming and having a water fight as wet as your hair and clothes are."

But Ruth was hurrying off to the kitchen and pretended not to hear, and the subject never came up again.

The family worked hard to get everything ready for Alph and Martha's marriage.

They had decided to have a traditional Jewish wedding, so Simon was making the poles and bows for the chuppah, and Eva and Rebeca were making the sheet that would cover the top and hang down on all four corners. During the ceremony, Alph and Martha would stand under the chuppah to symbolize their new home as husband and wife. Then they would exchange rings and recite from the Song of Songs. "I am my beloved's and my beloved is mine," and the rabbi would recite seven traditional blessings. After that Martha and Alph would drink some wine, then Alph would smash the glass under his right foot, and the guests would shout Mazel tov! And Alph and Martha would be married. But planning all of this took time.

The women in the family prepared food for the wedding feast, and Isaac spared no cost purchasing the wine. While the women worked, they talked of thing past and things to come.

One day when they were all working together, Eva said, "Isaac and I didn't go through all of this when we were married. With all the tradition, all this preparation, and all of the things to do, I sometimes wonder if Isaac and I are really married."

Rebeca laughed. "Believe me when I say, no matter how plain or simple your wedding was, you have been Isaac's wife for over twenty years, mother to his children, made his clothes, washed them, cooked his meals, even trimmed his beard. You are his wife many times over. The entire community knows that he loves you more than life itself. You are married. We all are.

It was quiet for a while, until someone started singing, and they continued until the work was done.

The day of the wedding arrived and everything was perfect. Even the weather cooperated. It was a beautiful, balmy day with a very slight breeze. The wedding started and everything went as planned until Plato got lonely. Everyone was at the wedding. No one was in sight, not a stranger, not a bird, or a wandering dog. So Plato decided the best thing for him to do was call his family. So, in his best and loudest voice he began to bray, and he brayed, and he brayed. Eva slipped out the back of the wedding, went over to Plato's pen, and scratched him behind the ears, and explained things to him. He decided to wait and quieted down. The wedding continued, and the incident was like it was planned as part of the ceremony, where Plato announced the wedding to the world.

After the wedding was over, Alph and Martha moved into the house that had been Mother Ruth's and their family community grew by one more family.

18

SAD TIMOTHY

Isaac loved the benches in front of his house. There used to be just two benches with room for two or maybe three men on each one. Then, Simon had made him three more. Now when he wants to relax of an evening, there is plenty of room for passersby to stop and chat for a while. One evening he sat on a bench by himself, chewing on a straw. Across the road from him stood old Plato, who was also chewing on some grass and watching him. Isaac crossed the road, scratched Plato behind the ears, and talked to him for a few minutes. Isaac wondered how much conversation this twenty-two year old donkey could understand. In his lifetime he'd certainly had enough people pour their heart out to him as they had scratched and petted him. He went back to his bench. He asked the next man that came by, "What's the oldest donkey you've ever known?" Over a period of several weeks, Isaac asked this question, and got answers that ranged from twelve to almost fifty years. The difference seemed to be the way the animals were fed and treated. The ones that were treated mostly like pets, worked some and fed well, but not so much they got too fat, lived the longest. Isaac figured that Plato may someday set an old-age record for donkeys.

Another day as Isaac sat on his bench; Timothy came up the road at a very slow pace. One hand gripping the other behind his back, and his head was down. He didn't notice Isaac until he was almost there.

"What's the matter Timothy?" said Isaac. "You look like you have a heavy heart."

"I do," said Timothy. "You are the patriarch of our community and the one I would like to ask for counsel, but you are involved in my problem. How can I ask you for advice?"

"I think you can," said Isaac. "Give me a try. I will disqualify myself if I can't give you unbiased advice." He knew what Timothy's problem was, but said no more to see what the young man would say.

So, Timothy poured his heart out to Isaac, this man whom he had known and admired all his life. "Your daughter Ruth and I are in love. She wants me to ask you for her hand in marriage, and I want to, but there are two major problems. One is that she is too young and still somewhat immature. The other is that I don't yet have a trade and am not making enough money to support us, especially if a child came along. My father works for you and you pay him well but I remember him and my mother talking about how difficult life was before he went to work for you. I can't learn from him because before he went to work for you he was doing the same thing I am doing now, working part time for the fish market or wherever he could find a day's work. I need to learn a trade before I get married."

"Timothy, what you tell me leads me to think you are a wise young man. Many young men in your position would jump right in, not thinking of the future, get married, and start having children before they thought of how they would feed them. Since my daughter is involved in this, I also have a stake in you learning a trade. Let me offer some suggestions. Simon and Alf are carpenters, Grandpa is a potter, Alph's new father-in-law is a cobbler, and I am a fisherman. You could start with any of us as an apprentice and you and Ruth could be betrothed in a couple of years. You are right about her age. She is too young to be married and although she may think she will die an old made if not married soon, she won't. Talk with Ruth about it and tell her that I won't give my blessing until you have a trade."

Timothy talked to Ruth. He told her about talking to Isaac and what Isaac said. He also told her that he thought Isaac was right, but she wasn't happy about it.

For a month Timothy looked at all of the trades and decided he would probably be the happiest as a fisherman and he would also have both Isaac and his father for support.

Isaac called a family meeting and invited Timothy for dinner and the meeting. After dinner, Isaac announced that Timothy had asked for Ruth's hand in marriage. He said he wasn't saying yes or no. There were to be two stipulations. First, Timothy would have to complete at least half of an apprenticeship for a trade and second, that Ruth must have passed her seventeenth birthday. So the marriage would have to wait for at least a year. In addition there would be no long walks alone or going off where no other adults were around.

Isaac said, "That is enough. You know what the restrictions are for and what they mean.

When Timothy and Ruth were alone, she complained about her father's restrictions. She wasn't at all happy with the plan. She said she knew of girls as young as fourteen that had gotten married and that seventeen was almost an old maid, but she agreed and told Timothy he had best get started in a trade. What Papa meant was that they couldn't have any privacy and that Alph and Martha's wedding was a big deal and they had no restrictions.

"As soon as I get started in a trade I will ask your father again," Said Timothy. "Maybe he will allow us to be betrothed."

Ruth still wasn't finished grumbling. "What we should do is run off to Jerusalem, get married, and live there."

"Ruth, I have never before seen this side of you," Timothy said. "I love you and want us to be married, but right now I think your father is very right. Not only do I need to provide for us, but you need to grow up. What you are saying sounds like a spoiled little girl. Your family is very close and when we are married we want to be part of it. Alph is my best friend and Martha is yours. Also, Martha was seventeen when they got married, and you are two years younger.

Ruth didn't say anything else. Timothy had never talked to her this way before. She wasn't sure he really did love her. Her face was red; she crossed her arms across her chest and stormed off without saying another word.

Three weeks went by and Ruth seemed to have returned to her normal self. Timothy was concentrating on getting started as an apprentice.

It was the fourth day of the week, and Isaac told Timothy he had work for him. So far, the only work Timothy had found was substitution work when one of Isaac and David's crew were sick. Today, one of the men had sent word that he wasn't feeling well. After the crew headed home that evening, David told Isaac, "We could put him to work every day if you wanted. If no one were absent he could mend nets or do something while the whole crew is working. He's a hard worker and I don't think he would sit around while the rest of us are out on the lake."

"I know," said Isaac, "I just want him to get the good and the bad. There will be fair-weather days and bad-weather days. It's more of a test than anything. I'm pretty sure this young man is going to be my son-in-law one day and I want him to be tough and faithful to the business."

"You mean this young man is Ruth's sweetheart?" David Said. "I didn't realize she was that old."

"Our children don't stay children long enough." said Isaac. "They grow up too fast. It was only yesterday, that Ruth and her friends were building castles in the sand by the river."

The subject dropped, but now there would be an extra man giving Timothy a little special attention to make a fisherman out of him.

The days and weeks went by and the man who had gotten sick got worse and had to quit. Isaac offered Timothy the job and asked him if he wanted to officially be and apprentice fisherman. He told him there would be a lot more to it than putting out nets and hauling in fish.

"If you will help me learn the business, I promise you, I will make you a first rate worker," Timothy said.

Timothy became the crew's official apprentice and the whole crew promised to help him learn the business.

One evening when the crew came in Isaac told him to get a stool and come with him. He sat him down by the fish counter and introduced him. He told the counter that Timothy was just starting and said, "I want him to sit in my place for a few days and help you. I would appreciate it if you could give him some tips."

At first Timothy couldn't begin to keep up with the fish as the workers were dumping them into the pond. The counter told him, "Don't try to count every individual fish. The men will dump one bucket of fish into the pond at a time. But when they dump them," the counter said, "they can go pretty fast, but they have to kind of let them flow out of the bucket. Then you can see how many there are."

By the end of that day's count he was beginning to get the knack of it. By the end of two weeks, he and the market's counter were hitting right on the same numbers. One day Timothy got a hundred fish more than the market's counter. The market counter said, "Well, you're new, you'll get the hang of it."

Timothy said, "No, I think I already have the hang of it. I might miss a few, maybe five or six but not one hundred."

"I'm never wrong," the fish counter said.

"I'm sorry sir." Timothy said, and started getting red faced, "But this time you are."

Isaac was standing beside him, and he and the fish counter started laughing. "That was a test," Isaac said. "And you passed. You'll make a fish counter."

Later that day, Isaac said to Timothy. "The fish counter told me that he thought you were first rate. I just thought I would pass that on to you. You see, the market buying the fish furnish a counter, and the fishing crew furnish one. Fishermen have used this system for many, many years. It insures an accurate count and keeps everyone happy. It almost never happens that there is a discrepancy. If there is, the two counters work it out and no one ever knows it. It's their job and they have to be right and agree."

The next day Alph met Timothy on the way home from work.

"How is it going Timothy?"

"I don't know." he said. "Working in the boat is fine. Although I need a lot more practice, I can cast a net pretty well, and mend them, but there is so much more when you are running the crew and that's what he seems to want me to do. He also wants me to learn how to haggle with the market on the fish price when we settle up." And then he told Alph about the fish counting.

"Father may be hard on you," Alph said. "But he wants you to learn the fish business. Anyone can catch fish, but running a business with a partner and a dozen employees to be concerned with, is a big responsibility. Father likes you, and wants you to do well, especially since you are going to be the father of his grandchildren." Alph laughed and said, "Timothy, fathers want to pass on their businesses to their sons. Papa's son is a carpenter and already has a business. You will be marrying his daughter, putting you in line as the second son. He won't tell you that, but it's what is going to happen. If you love the business and you love

Papa, don't say anything. Just go with it. You will probably be his partner one day."

They smiled at each other, and nothing else was ever said.

Alph asked how he and Ruth were getting along. And then Timothy unloaded Ruth's outburst on him.

Alph laughed and said, "You have seen the dark side of my little sister. She has a temper at times, but when she is sweet, she is really sweet, which is most of the time. You will find that if you just leave her alone, she will work it out. She really doesn't want to run off. She will be back to normal in no time."

Timothy grinned and said, "She already is."

19

BUILDING

Isaac went out the back door of his house and stood with his arms crossed looking at the courtyard formed by the family's houses. They had paved the courtyard with basalt blocks and left Mother Ruth's garden open, but since no one had planted it, it was overgrown with weeds and the strip across the back was covered with weeds.

Alph and Martha had come over to visit and they and Eva were standing in the kitchen talking. Isaac called to them, "You people come out here and look."

They all went outside. They all looked around and Alph said, "What are we supposed to look at?"

"What do you see?"

Alph looked for another minute and then said, "Well, we are in the courtyard, but there are more weeds than anything. Mother Ruth's garden has gone to ruin. I see the backs of Simon and Mary's house, the woodshop, an empty space with more weeds and the back of your house.

"It's not exactly a beautiful garden anymore is it?" Isaac scratched his chin. "The empty space is ours. Now imagine this. Another house built across the back open space, and a couple of rooms connecting it to Eva and I's house? Up here in the front, Mother Ruth's old home is remodeled and made new. The garden could be rimmed with stone and we built a basalt lined fire pit."

"It sound nice," said Alph. "But also pretty ambitious."

""Yes it is," Isaac agreed. "But in time to come, Timothy and Ruth are going to need a home, Simon and Mary already have a son, and I hope that someday you mother and I will become grandparents. Right now, you and I are experiencing very prosperous times in our business. Now would be the most ideal time to build."

"Father, I think you're right. Our business is doing very well, but if the Roman administrators change we could lose our contract with them. I think we should do it while we can. I can pay for a new house across the back for Martha and I. We are planning on several children and will need room."

"This sounds good to me," Isaac said. "And I can finance the rest."

Until now neither of the women had said anything. Eva spoke. "If you men are going to build this city you are talking about, who is going to clean and scrub it?"

Alph said, "There are five parts to it. Simon and I are responsible for the wood shop, and he and Mary for their house. Martha and I will be responsible for our house, you and Papa for yours, and Timothy and Mary for theirs. It would be the same if we were all separated by distance, but this way we can help each other."

"I like it," said Martha. "And my parents would be right behind us; everyone only a few steps away"

"It does make sense," Eva said. "But, there are a lot of details to work out. Timothy and Ruth aren't even married yet and they won't have much money for a good while, and Simon and Mary don't even know we are talking about it.

Alph can get Simon's opinion on the project tomorrow," Isaac said. "And I will talk to Timothy."

The next day at work Alph talked to Simon about the project, and he was excited about it. He said, "The back of our house and woodshop will both be on the courtyard. I want to cut a door from both of them out onto the courtyard."

Isaac got to work extra early the next day and Timothy was already there. He said, "Timothy, Let's sit on the log over there by the wooded area." After they were seated, Isaac said, I have worked you hard and put you in situations where you had no experience, just to see how you handled it. You have done very well. If you could figure it out, you did it, and if you couldn't you came and asked me. That is just what you should have done. I've told you before, almost anyone can catch a fish, but running a business is something different. I'm proud of you. Now, for the big question; how do you and Ruth stand on your desire to get married?"

Timothy said, "We want to be married more than anything. I love Ruth very much and am proud of her. She has come to understand why we couldn't marry when she wanted. She was just excited about Alph and Martha, but I think she is ready now."

"Have you spoken to your Parents?"

"Yes," said Timothy, "But my being married to his boss's daughter, makes Papa uncomfortable, even though you are friends."

"I understand," said Isaac, "and I will have a talk with him before the wedding. Don't say anything to him now, but you could be his boss someday, however, knowing you, I think you will work it out. Do you have any plans for dinner tomorrow evening?"

"No sir," he said.

"Good," said Isaac. "And don't call me Sir. The rest of the men just call me Isaac or boss when they are clowning around. You do the same for now and after the wedding you can change it to Papa."

Alph woke early the next morning and slipped out of the house while Martha was still sleeping. He wanted to take a walk and think about the news he had heard from Jerusalem. Word had reached them that Jesus had been arrested and taken before Pilate. The people were saying that Pilate seemed to be afraid of Jesus. The religious leaders however were stirred into frenzy over the things Jesus had said. They called it blasphemy. Pilate finally turned him over to the Roman soldiers and they crucified him on a cross just outside of town. They wanted his blood. It was said that he would be back in three days. Pilate had the tomb sealed and guarded just in case the disciples wanted to steal his body and lay some claim that he had risen.

The people who were telling the story said that on the morning of the third day Jesus did rise from the dead. They even knew people who had seen him around town after his death. There were so many stories being told that it was difficult separating fiction from fact.

Capernaum was buzzing with the story. People who had heard Jesus preach and believed in him knew that surely it was true. Jesus must really be the Messiah. But if Jesus really is the Messiah – Alph wondered – if he really did die and come back to life, what will happen next? As Alph walked down toward the sea, he veered off his usual path to where there was a grove of trees. The lower side of the trees opened onto a sandy beach, and Alph sat down on an old log at the edge of the trees. A man was frying fish over an open fire on the beach, and out on the sea, some other men were rowing a fishing boat toward him.

Alph looked hard at the men in the boat and realized that one of them was Simon Peter, one of the men Jesus had picked to be an apostle. Alph was a little surprised to see him there, but as he looked he realized that the rest of the men in the boat were also apostles of Jesus. The boat appeared to be empty – there were no fish in sight. The man on the beach called to them and asked what they had caught. The men shouted back that they hadn't caught anything. Then the man on the beach did the strangest thing. He told the fishermen to put their nets on the other side of the boat. What does it matter what side of the boat the net is on, Alph wondered. And then, suddenly, the men started shouting – and fish were jumping into the net, so many that the men couldn't even pull the net in.

Alph looked back at the man on the beach and realized who it was. It was Jesus, and Alph stood up. Just then Jesus turned toward him, and he got the same feeling he had at the wedding in Cana. Then he turned away.

"Bring in some of your fish," Jesus said. "Join me for breakfast." So they did.

Alph stood there for a few minutes and continued to watch. He wasn't sure if he stayed there out of fear, or respect, or both. When he finally did slip away in the direction from which he had come, he didn't tell anyone what had happened, until he found his father and then he told him everything he had seen and heard, and of the feeling he had.

After everyone had eaten that evening, Isaac called the family meeting to order. When everyone was ready, he announced, "Timothy has asked for Ruth's hand in marriage." He stopped, then grinned as he went ahead and said, "I know you are all surprised."

Everyone started laughing and Ruth covered her face.

Isaac went on. He said, "Eva and I have discussed the matter and I have talked with Timothy's parents, and both they and us are agreed that they are ready. Many things are happening right now. Ruth's seventeenth birthday is approaching, Timothy is doing very well learning the business end of fishing, and we have a huge family undertaking with the construction we have planned. When it is completed Alph and Martha will be moving into their new home and we will remodel Mother Ruth's old home and make it new for Timothy and Ruth. Therefore, Timothy and Ruth are officially betrothed, and will be married in the spring right after Ruth's seventeenth birthday.

After everyone settled down Alph told the family what he had seen and heard on the beach. "There is no question!" he said excitedly, "Jesus is the Christ, the Messiah. I saw him. If we believe in him, and in his teachings, we will have eternal life. He is supposed to be dead, but I saw him with my own eyes, there on the beach, with his disciples. Papa and I are going to study all that we can find of what he has taught. After we have studied, we will have some family meetings and teach you all what we have learned.

He paused for a moment, and then reached out and pulled Martha up with him. Now I have another announcement, Martha and I are going to be parents."

With all that was going on and all of the announcements the crowd was stunned. They were quiet for a moment and then everyone started applauding.

The sun was getting low and the Sabbath was rapidly approaching. The women quickly cleaned the table and Alph and Martha left to go tell her parents all the news and Timothy and Ruth did the same with instructions from Mother that Ruth was to be home before dark, which didn't set well with Ruth, but she kept her silence.

The two grandfathers, along with Simon and Isaac, went out to the benches while Eva, Mary, Martha, and little John sat and visited.

20

MORE CHANGES

With Martha expecting a baby and a wedding being planned for Timothy and Ruth there wasn't much time to be wasted with the construction project. Isaac found a man anxious to sell a team of mules and a wagon at a very good price and bought them to haul building materials. When he brought them home he parked the wagon by Plato's donkey cart. Then he called Eva to talk to Plato while he opened the gate and crossed his fingers before putting the mules in the lot with the little donkey. At first the animals just looked at each other. Then the mules walked over to the far side of the lot from Plato and stood there together. Plato ignored them and continued to eat his hay as if nothing different was happening.

Isaac put some hay out for the mules in their chosen spot as Plato watched. When Isaac finished, Plato raised his head and brayed one long trumpet blast, looked for a minute and then went back to his hay. Isaac and Eva had no idea what that meant but it seemed peaceful. They gave the mules buckets to eat their grain from, and all was peaceful. He and Eva kept a close eye on them for a while, but everything seemed okay. There was one good – sized wooden watering trough that they all drank out of but at different times. As time went by the mules lived on their side of the lot and Plato on his. They didn't fraternize, but there was no confrontation.

Everyone worked on the project when they could, but always with at least two men together. Isaac hired some of his fishermen who wanted to work extra hours but with Simon, Andrew, James, and John the fishermen, away telling people about Jesus, the fish market was keeping them pretty busy. Alph and Simon made the plans and instructed everyone as to what was needed. They took the mule wagon up to the forest at the foot of the mountain and selected trees, cut them, and brought them down for timbers and beams, other trips were made to haul basalt from the mines. It would take a good bit for floors, the foundation and the courtyard. Plato and his cart were used to haul grass for thatching, poles, and mud from Grandpa's clay pit. Sometimes the mules and Plato were used to haul the same thing. When they were, Plato always hurried to stay ahead of the mules. He wanted them to know which hauling rig was the best and most important. On occasion he would run if necessary to get ahead and stay there.

After the heavy hauling was finished Grandpa asked Isaac if he and Grandfather could use the mules to take a load of pottery to Jerusalem. Isaac said it would be fine, and if he could get a good price for it, sell the mule team and wagon also.

Simon and Alph had just finished rebuilding a one horse Roman chariot. It wasn't nearly as large and heavy as the regular two horse chariots, and they wondered how difficult it would be to connect it to the back of the wagon. It proved to be a fairly simple task to connect them, and the load of pots was not heavy.

"That whole load isn't half the weight we were hauling on many of our building material loads," Alph said. "Two mules will have no problem pulling the load. And I will go along with you and deliver the chariot to the Jerusalem Barracks."

Grandpa had enough pottery made to fill the wagon. He and Grandfather loaded it and stuffed straw around all of the pots to keep them from breaking. They used one corner of the bed for their food and sleeping bed rolls.

It was partly cloudy the morning they left, but this time of year there was usually very little rain. It did rain a little however, but the showers were light, and nothing to be feared. But, on the second day of the trip, the thunder rolled, lightening cracked, and it poured rain. All of the little streams they had to cross were swollen. The mules were trudging along in the downpour, and shaking with every clap of thunder and flash of light. Alph was afraid they might break and run, but they held their poise. About mid-day it seemed the summer storm had set in to stay, when they came upon a young family with an expectant mother and two small children. The young mother seemed very young to have two small children and another on the way. They were all miserably soaked with water, and while Alph was talking to them, the young father was the only one that was not crying.

Alph got out his bed roll, and put the family in the chariot. Grandpa and Grandfather both volunteered their bed rolls and Alph was able to get enough over them to shed most of the water. The father said he had lost his job and they were headed to Jericho where their family lived. By evening they had reached a stream too deep for them to cross, and it had quit raining, so they made camp for the night. They put all of their food together and rationed it out, holding some back for the next few days.

By morning the stream was down, it had quit raining, and by mid-morning they were mostly dried out. By that evening they reached Jericho and dropped their new-found friends at their family home. They had a good meal, got fresh supplies, and started up the mountain the next morning.

When they reached Jerusalem, they went to the market place and found one large shop that said they would take everything at the price Grandpa was asking.

Before they left Grandpa said, "Do you know anyone interested in buying our mules and wagon?"

"If the price is right, I might be interested," said the owner.

Grandfather pretended to be thinking for a few minutes, and then gave him one and a half times the price Isaac paid for it.

The shop owner had a hard time hiding his enthusiasm, and then said, "I will take them."

They made arrangements to get the chariot out to the Roman barracks and as soon as Alph settled up, they were on their way.

"We have not taken into consideration the difference in prices between Capernaum and Jerusalem," Grandpa said. "We could have gotten a lot more if we had asked more and haggled with them."

"We got what we wanted," said Alph, "and the next time we will look around Jerusalem and check prices before we offer our goods."

Grandfather said, "I feel guilty for not knowing better. We lived near here, and I should have known there was a price difference between here and up in the country."

When they got home Isaac suggested that the two grandfathers might go into the mule trader business but they said they thought not.

A few weeks had gone by while all of the building materials were being stockpiled, but they were finally ready to start. The foundation was set and leveled, and construction began. Alph and Simon closed the woodshop, and Isaac took half of his crew and left the other half with David to do the best they could in supplying fish. Eva, Martha, Rebecca, Ruth and some friends fed the men while they worked and kept the trash and construction debris cleaned up. In less than a month the building was complete.

There was one room at the end of Isaac's house that had only an outside door opening into the courtyard. Isaac said it was for a special purpose but said nothing more. No one pushed him about what that purpose was but Isaac told Alph and Simon that he would pay them to build him some shelves, a bed, a table and a couple of chairs to put in it. It seemed obvious that it was for someone special.

When they were back at the shop Simon said, "What is this special room for? It looks like Isaac is setting it up to rent to travelers for the night," and then laughed.

Alph said, "My guess would be that he is building and furnishing it for Edfu, but I don't know."

Alph and Martha moved into the new house, and Mother Ruth's old house was cleaned and remodeled so that after the wedding Timothy and Ruth could move into it. Now it was time for wedding preparations. Isaac had made a pretty good profit over the last few years and had saved his money, but by the time the building was complete and the wedding was over, he wouldn't have much left. That was O.K. He would have taken care of his family, planned for their future and surrounded himself and Eva with them. Everything was good and Grandfather Isaac was a happy man.

Ruth's wedding was pretty much a repeat of Alph's and came off with no problems. This time however, Eva went over to the donkey, sat down by him, and had a talk with her pet. She talked to him in a soft voice, "Plato, before the wedding starts, you are to promise me that you are going to be quiet. If you are not, I will hold back your special treats for a month. You are to be quiet during all of the activities. No one has abandoned you and a new young couple will be moving in just across the street from you." She touched his nose with her finger and said, "Do we understand each other?"

There wasn't a peep out of him the whole day.

Timothy and Ruth moved into their home, and Ruth seemed to transform from a somewhat rebellious teenager to a young married woman almost overnight. Isaac and Eva went from being a family with a teenage daughter to a childless couple. But, with a daughter-in-law soon expecting her first child, that lonely status would be short lived.

One Sabbath afternoon, Isaac was sitting in front of his house. As he looked up the road he saw a man walking toward him. He wondered, now who could that man be, traveling on the Sabbath? It certainly isn't a Jew. Then as the man got closer, he could tell that he was a black man. Could that be? Could it be Edfu? He'd said he might surprise Isaac one day. Then as the man got closer he could tell. It was Edfu. Isaac got up and shouted his name. Edfu quickened his pace until he was in the yard. The men exchanged greetings and Edfu said, "I thought I would have to look all over Capernaum for you and here you are."

Isaac invited his old friend in and called Eva. She didn't seem as surprised as Isaac thought she might be. She had known when Isaac wanted that extra room what he had in mind. She said, "I have had a feeling ever since I met you in Jerusalem that we would see you here one day. Do you plan to stay?"

Edfu said, "I am through with camels. One day I was happy with my job and the next day I just decided I was tired of traveling and wanted a home. Do you think Capernaum would accept an old camel driver into its citizenry?"

"I think we would," said Isaac. "Come with me." Isaac led Edfu out the back of his home into the courtyard and opened the door to the room behind his house. Then he said, "Come in, Edfu, This is your home for as long as you want it. When we built onto our home I knew in my heart that someday you would be here. I added this room just for you."

Edfu didn't know what to say, so he just stood there repeating, "Yes, yes, yes."

And so, Edfu became the newest citizen of Capernaum. The story of Isaac's trip to Egypt had been told so many times that it seemed everyone in Capernaum already knew Edfu although it took him some time to get to know them. He, Grandfather Daniel and Grandpa Nikos, all in their fifties, became friends quickly. Edfu was fascinated with Daniel's fiery furnace and the shaping of iron into tools. Grandfather asked him if he would be interested in a job and Edfu said that he supposed he would. His money wasn't going to last forever and he needed a way to support himself. Although Edfu was much older than young apprentices learning a trade or skill, it was something he really liked and wanted. He had a good eye for the color of the red hot metal when he was working it; how and where to bend it, how to quench it to make it hard and draw it out to soften it. Daniel only need show him once and he would remember.

Since hearing Jesus' sermon up on the mountain Isaac and Alph had pledged to one another to start praying to God at least once a day. Isaac chose dinner time with Eva and whoever else had gathered with them for the evening meal for one of his prayers. The other was a private one when his head was on the pillow, when he and Eva had gotten quiet for the night and it was only he and God listening to the words in his mind before he dropped off to sleep. Any other special time or when he thought he needed to speak to God he would offer another prayer. His thank you prayers always included his family and friends and Jesus Christ for the redemption of his sins. Isaac was a good man and he knew that he was the senior leader of not only his family but of the community and he also knew that Alph would be following him in that position.

Words had come ahead that some Pharisees were traveling around the country with Roman Soldiers, pretending to know who the troublemakers in each community were. They pretended to know who the people were that advocated throwing over the Roman Empire. Their personal agendas however were to get rid of all of the followers of "The Way," those who believed in Jesus Christ and followed his teachings. Isaac had heard that these people were coming to Capernaum.

One morning Alph stopped by on his way to work just to visit with his parents for a few minutes. There was a knock on the door, and two Pharisees and a centurion stood there. The centurion said, "We are looking for a fisherman named Isaac and his son, a carpenter named Alph. Are you them?"

Isaac spoke up and said, "I am Isaac. How may I help you?"

The centurion said to the two Pharisees, "I will question these men while you go up the street and check on some others. We will gather together with the soldiers and those who need to come with us and take them all to Jerusalem."

As soon as the others left the centurion smiled and said to Alph, "Do you remember me?"

"I remember you," Alph said, "but I can't remember where we met."

"I am Atticus, one of the soldiers that stayed overnight with you when you broke the wheel on your donkey cart," he said, "I was just a foot soldier then but decided to make a career in the military and went to officer training school. How did you and your father get your names on this list?"

"It is because we believe in Jesus Christ, God's son," he said. "The Pharisees want to be rid of us."

"I was stationed in Jerusalem when John was preaching and baptizing." Atticus said, "I went down to hear John several times and was baptized. If I take you to Jerusalem on these trumped up charges the court will find you guilty of being trouble makers and beat you with a whip before turning you lose to come home with bloody backs. I am going up the street. See that both of you disappear for the rest of the day. Go fishing with your father and stay away until dark. I will give them some wild story and they won't be back here for months and maybe never. Rome is getting tired of these useless trips to satisfy your Pharisees. It is good to see you Alph and I hope we meet again now that I am in charge of the detachment here in Capernaum."

"Thank you Atticus. Please come by and meet my family and have dinner with us, my wife is a good cook."

"I will," Atticus said, "and your wife is a good cook. It shows on you. Good bye Alph and watch who you proclaim your faith in front of."

Alph and Isaac stopped by the carpenter shop and told Simon where Alph would be, and then they spread word around before going fishing. Five of their friends came down to the dock. They offered to volunteer their services without pay on the boats for the day and Simon closed the carpenter shop and got together a spontaneous group of hunters to go up stream for a day of trapping along the river.

About mid-afternoon Atticus and the Pharisees who were with him gathered their soldiers and left for Jerusalem. It seems that none of the men they wanted were at home today.

21

MARTHA'S TIME

It has been well over a year since Alph and Martha were married. Their new home had to be furnished, and Alph has spent most of his free time building bedroom and kitchen furniture but now that Martha is expecting a baby, he's concentrating on nursery furniture.

One morning, Isaac had just left for work, and Eva was cleaning up after breakfast when Martha appeared in the door, her hands held in the small of her back. It was obvious her labor had started. Eva went out the back door and shouted for Ruth. She came immediately and Eva told her it was time. "Go get the midwife and then try to get Alph and Isaac before the boats go out," she ordered.

Ruth left, and Eva didn't much more than get Martha settled in her bed before the mid-wife was there. Alph was right behind Ruth, followed by the mid-wife, then Isaac, Nikos, Daniel, Simon, Mary and Edfu. Ruth told Alph he knew where to go and said, "Take your parade of men out to the benches with you and we will call you if you're needed, but don't count on it."

Alph had been on the benches with Simon when John was born but this was his child, his baby, and it was different. Isaac had been through this before as had Nikos and Daniel but this was Isaac's first grandchild and then there was poor Edfu who had no idea what was happening. Isaac told Edfu that the men's job was to wait and wait and wait. After four or five hours Alph went into the kitchen and started making sandwiches.

Simon came in, and Alph said, "Get some wine from the cupboard and see if you can find some cups to drink from."

While they were eating they thought they heard a noise but it was a false alarm.

Finally Ruth came out with a big smile. "It's a girl she said."

But while they were still talking about her, Mary came out and said, "It's another girl. You have twins."

After another terrible time of waiting Eva came out.

She said, "You can come and look but are to be quiet, the girls are asleep."

The women had put the babies in the cradle foot to foot since it was large enough for both of them.

The next day Martha and Alph presented the babies with a string around one of the girls' ankles, for there was no way to tell them part.

Martha said, "Their names will be Miriam, with the string, and Maria."

The first few days were busy with all the visitors coming by to see the babies. Twins weren't unheard of, but were uncommon. Eva and Rebecca took the responsibility of caring for the girls while Martha got plenty of rest. Their greatest concern was trying to figure out how to tell them apart. The string was on Miriam's ankle but she couldn't wear it forever.

When the babies were four days old the grandmothers were sitting on the edge of Martha's bed and the three women were cooing over them, playing with them, and trying to get them to smile. To them they were precious dolls.

Suddenly Rebecca started laughing and said, "I think I know how to tell them apart." She was holding Maria and said, "Maria has a very small heart shaped birthmark behind one ear. See if Miriam has one.

Eva said, "Well that isn't going to work. Miriam has one behind her left ear."

Rebecca said, "Are you sure it's not her right ear."

Eva said, "No. It's her left ear."

Then Rebecca really started laughing. She said, "The twins aren't identical. They are mirror images of each other. Maria's birthmark is behind her right ear."

When the twins got older, it would be consternation to them. If one of them got into trouble, Martha would reach for the ear of the closest girl almost pulling it off to see which one it was, but for now it was a sure identification and a joke to be told to the rest of the family. Miriam was right and Maria was left. As they got older it was discovered that Miriam, with the right side birthmark, really was right handed and Maria, with the left side birthmark was left handed. They were right and left identical twins, for in every other way they were exactly the same.

It wasn't long until they were able to roll themselves over, and were soon crawling, and then taking their first wobbly steps just before their first birthday. Alph was so proud of them he could bust, but Martha was wishing she could move them back to the crawling stage. They were into everything, and every evening when Alph came in from work they would come running and each one would tackle a leg. A couple of times when Alph wasn't watching for them they took him off of his feet. The girls thought it was great sport but Alph learned to be ready for the attack.

By the time they were two they were into everything. Their Cousin John, Simon and Mary's son, was four and lived next door. The three of them were together most of the time and Uncle Edfu and Grandfather Isaac called them the terrible trio. When Isaac and Edfu were playing with them the five were constantly in trouble with their mothers and Grandmother Eva.

One day, around lunch time, Alph told Simon he was really getting hungry. He said that Martha had made a stew that smelled wonderful, and he had yet to taste it. He said, "I think I'll go home for lunch and get some."

Simon said, "Good. Let's close the shop for a long lunch. I'll see you back here after a while."

While Alph, Martha and the girls were eating lunch, the girls were chattering away as usual while Alph watched and smiled.

Martha said, "What are you smiling about?"

Alph said, "I was just thinking. In another ten years these two are going to start noticing the boys and being boys they will be a year or two behind them. It will be two on one and the poor boys won't stand a chance."

Martha hit him and said, "Shame on you. It will be your job to watch those boys and see that your daughters remain good young ladies. You aren't supposed to feel sorry for the boys. You are supposed to make sure they are afraid of you, and on their best behavior."

Alph stood up to leave before he laughed and said, "I'll give them a few tips," and then ran out the door before Martha could get a good swing at him.

Alph and Simon had no more than returned to the shop before Atticus came in. Alph greeted him and said, "Atticus my good friend. What brings you here today? Do you need something built?" You know we do the best woodwork in Galilee."

"I know you do," said Atticus. "You really do. That's what has me worried. Tetrarch Herod Antipas with all of his building and construction has decided to build him a new capital where he can sit and rule over Galilee. It is going to be located just this side of Magdala and will have a palace for him with paved streets and a wall around it. Its name will be Tiberius, after Emperor Tiberius, and it will be second in size only to Jerusalem. I have been told to gather the best carpenters and stone masons I can find and encourage them – with force if I have to – to move to this new city of Tiberius. There will be homes for them with very good wages and they will be expected to stay there after the city is finished. I am already running into opposition. It is said that there is a cemetery there and no Jew wants anything to do with the project if it means building over a Jewish cemetery. I am pretty sure that you want nothing to do with it since you are both Jewish and followers of The Way. I need some help in finding a reason you should be disqualified."

"That should be no problem," said Simon. "Alph and I have a contract with Rome to build and repair their carts and chariots in the region of Galilee. We can't move to this city of Tiberius and still honor our contract with Rome."

"Why didn't I think of that?" Atticus slapped his own forehead. "I just received a letter telling me to take my wooden equipment to you for repairs. I guess I jumped to a conclusion thinking I was going to have to pressure my friends. Good. Very good."

"If it's all that good, you are way over due for dinner with Martha and me." Alph said, "Let me talk to her, and we want you to join us one evening."

Atticus said, "Good again. I have wanted to visit you and see how families of 'The way' live. I may want to start looking for a wife. Good day my friends. I will stop here again in a few days and you can come to the soldier's barracks any time. Just tell them you are a friend of Centurion Atticus and they will find me. I do carry a little weight there." And he laughed as he waved good bye.

That evening Alph asked Martha if they could have Atticus over for their evening meal.

"I think that would be a grand idea, just give me a day's notice."

"What about the end of the week, the day before Sabbath, Alph said?"

"Fine. Does he have a lady friend?" Martha said.

"I don't think so," Said Alph, "But I will ask."

The next day Alph went by the barracks where Atticus had his office. He told him of the plans and Atticus said that he was looking forward to meeting his family.

Then he said, "I have some good news but also some bad. I just received notice that I have been given a promotion. I don't yet know what it is but I have been recalled to Rome. I am afraid I am being replaced as Centurion. It seems that Just as I am getting settled, and making new friends, I get pulled out and moved."

"If the army is to be your career, that is good," said Alph. "But, I am so sorry to see you leave. It seems like we have been friends for a long time, even though we have seen little of each other. Do you know anything about your new position?"

"Nothing." said Atticus. "I do know the man that is taking my place. We went to officer's school and served together in Jerusalem. We went together to hear John the Baptist, and he too was baptized. He is a good man. I will be here until he arrives to replace me and will introduce you before I leave."

The men said their goodbyes and promised to see each other later that week.

Having nothing else to say Alph went home and told Martha.

Atticus was prompt on the evening of the dinner. He was neatly trimmed and in his officer's dress-uniform. The girls were wide eyed when they saw him and stayed close to their mother without saying a word. For them, that was almost unheard of.

Miriam took hold of Martha's sleeve and pulled her down to whisper in her ear. "What do we call him?"

"I don't know," said Martha. "Ask your father."

"Why don't you call him Officer Atticus," said Alph.

"That would be fine, "Atticus said. "That's what almost everyone calls me."

"Then why does Papa just call him Atticus?" Maria said.

"It is because they are good friends." Martha told her.

"Oh." Miriam and Maria nodded their head together, and it seemed to be settled.

When they settled down to dinner, Alph asked everyone to bow their heads so he could say a blessing before they ate. When all was quiet and the girls were bowed with their hands folded Alph said, "Father in heaven, thank you for our friends and our family, for the world that you have created, for the love that Jesus so strongly preached, and the forgiveness of our sins for which he died. Please bless the food that Martha has prepared. Bless our friend Atticus who is now leaving us and bless his future. Thank you for sending your son Jesus. Bless us that we might learn and understand his teaching. Amen!"

The girls said together, "Amen."

After the meal they visited for a while. When it came time for Atticus to leave, he praised Martha's meal and said that he wished he could stay in Capernaum. He said, "Your friendship is something rare when you are serving in the army. Almost all of your friends are those who are also serving. I am envious of you and hope to someday have a home like yours." Then he excused himself and left to return to the barracks.

After he left Alph said that he didn't envy the life of a soldier.

Another day Abe came over carrying a leather bag. He told Alph he had made it from some leftover scraps, and Alph could use it to carry his lunch in. He said, "Just don't show it off to everyone or I'll never get done making them. The only person except Martha who ever paid attention to it was Simon, and he didn't need one. The shop was right behind his house and he just stepped through a door for lunch.

One evening Alph came home carrying some boards. He went out into the courtyard and arranged them like a big box in one corner of the garden. When Martha asked what they were for he said it was going to be a surprise for the children. Every evening Alph brought home his lunch bag full of sand from the beach next to the dock. Within three weeks Alph had a pretty sizable pile of sand inside that box. He smoothed it out and called the girls. He showed them how to make roads in it with the little blocks of wood he had brought home and how to make Egyptian pyramids, houses and other things. The girls were delighted.

The next evening Alph came in from work to find the girls standing naked on their table with Martha washing them down. She was not happy and let Alph know it. She told him he had a choice. He could clean the sand off of the girls and out of their hair every day, wash the sand out of their clothes, and clean up the sand they tracked into the house; all of this to be done daily and sometimes twice or he could destroy his sand box and mix the sand into the dirt in the garden. Then she said, "But before you do that you had better go over and apologize to Mary. John is probably as filthy as the girls."

His answer was something like a soft "Yes dear," and then he went over to Simon and Mary's where Mary was trying to get John clean and Simon was laughing at her.

She said, "If you came over to apologize, your apology is accepted if you will get my husband out of here. He thinks this is funny. The two of you can build a wall around your sandbox."

When they went out into the courtyard, Isaac and Edfu were standing there talking. Alph started pulling up the boards and Simon got a hoe and began mixing the sand into the dirt.

Isaac said, "What are you men doing with me and the children's sand box."

Simon handed him the hoe and said, "Here! If this was your sandbox you can help with its demise."

Then Alph explained the women's edict. Isaac started laughing at him and it got worse on every turn of the story. When it was all over, Isaac didn't help the situation. He waited until everyone was together and then asked the children where their sandbox was. Maria got excited and said that Papa and Uncle Simon tore it all up. Then Miriam said, "And Mother was mad at everyone. She made me and Maria stay inside while they tore up everything."

One day at lunch time the fishermen were eating their lunches when a little buff colored stray dog came up to the dock. He was cute, friendly and begging everyone for handouts. Several of the men obliged him until he was full. It soon became a habit and he was there every day for lunch. Isaac told the men that if they didn't quit they would never get rid of him. So, they did quit, but the little dog just waited until they went back out to sea, and then he dug their left overs out of the trash pit and had a feast, but left a mess when he was done. Usually he was gone in the evening, but one evening, Timothy was the last to leave and the dog followed him home. Timothy tried to chase the dog off all the way to the house, but the dog thought it was a game.

Timothy asked Isaac how he thought they could get rid of the dog but Isaac said, "The children are out there playing with it now, and they and the dog are having a wonderful time. If you kill it you will be the most hated man in the neighborhood. See if you can get one of the men at the dock to take it home."

That didn't work. Everyone thought he was a cute pup, but no one wanted him.

Three days later, the dog was still following Timothy home. He would follow Timothy to work and then go back home when the boats went out. At lunch time he was back to eat, but when Timothy got home from work, he would be there playing with the children. To make things worse Ruth named him Buff because of his color. Now with a name, Buff had pretty well claimed himself a new home with no way to get rid of him. He was Timothy's dog.

The children's boundary was the lower side of John's house. They weren't to go any farther down the street than there. The girls had made it past their fifth birthday, and John was seven, so one day they decided among themselves that they had been restricted long enough, and they were now old enough to explore. Of course Buff would be along to protect them. Three children and a dog walked down beside the fish market and started up the river without anyone noticing them.

They reached the old swimming hole where Alph had caught Ruth and her friend swimming. Maria waded down into the water and then slipped down into the deep water. John and Miriam found a long stick by the side of the river and pushed the end out to Maria. Maria got hold of it but couldn't pull herself out. In fact, she was having a hard time keeping her head above water. Buff knew something was wrong and started running back toward the fish market yapping as loud as he could.

In the meantime, the girls had been missed and the first thing Alph thought of was the river. He started running and just little way up the path met Buff, barking. Buff turned around and went running back toward the swimming hole with Alph running after him. As he came into sight of the swimming hole, John yelled, "Maria fell in and can't get out."

Alph waded down into the water, got a girl under each arm and pushed John ahead of him. Maria was sputtering and had taken in a lot of water so Alph sat on a big rock with Maria face down over his lap, patting her on the back. She coughed up and spit water for a few minutes and then started crying. Alph picked up both girls and carried them home with John and Buff following along.

When they got home, Mary took John by the arm and said, "Did you take those girls down to the river?"

Before John could answer Alph said, "It's not John's fault. I think it was probably a conspiracy between them. No one was forced or dragged down there. They are all three to blame, and if it hadn't been for Buff I may not have found them in time.

Mary took John into the house and Martha and Alph took the girls home. As soon as they got into the house Martha said, "Miriam, you go to your room and Maria, you are to go to me and Papa's room."

Maria said, "That's no fun."

"We won't even be able to talk," Miriam wailed.

Martha said, "I don't mean for it to be fun. I want you to stay in there and think about what could have happened. Do you know that Papa Isaac had a sister that drowned when he was a little boy? You will stay in that room until I decide you have learned to obey and not go where you are told not to go. And I may give Buff your dinner for helping to save you. Do you understand?"

"Yes mother."

Now Buff had a new home for sure.

One day it was really cold outside, and John and the twins were running through the houses. This wasn't appreciated by the mothers, and Grandmother Eva told them to go outside to play. They said it was too cold. Then she said, "Go to my kitchen where I am baking bread. I have a fire going and it is warm there."

"What can we do in there?" John whined.

"Play that stick game that your grandfather taught you." Grandmother said.

"We don't have any sticks." Maria argued.

"Then go out and find some!" Grandmother said.

"Where?" Miriam said.

Eva was at the end of her patience. She said, "Take Buff with you and follow him until you see some. If that doesn't work, sit on Grandpa's benches out front until I tell you that you can come in. Is that clear?"

They got the message and left without another word. In a short time they were back with some sticks and played by the fire until Alph came to get them for dinner.

Before he left Alph said, "How has your day gone, Mother?"

That was a bad question.

It was the day Alph received an extended education on the day to day lives of wives, mothers, and grandmothers.

22

EDFU AND A FIREWOOD TRIP

There is nothing to make a person feel more worthless, than to know he is not needed, and Edfu certainly felt he was out of place, not needed, and even a burden to the family he loved and wanted to be with. For most of the last two decades he knew that his time on earth would have ended, had it not been for the grace of his good friend Isaac. Now, he had been invited to come and stay with Isaac and his family, but he knew that even now he was a burden. Nikos was a very good professional potter, and Daniel a metal smith. But he, Edfu, was just there. Isaac had made him his own little room in which to live, Eva washed his clothes and fed him, and he did nothing in return. He was treated very well; even the children called him Uncle Edfu. But, he was doing nothing to earn his keep.

The market was cleaning the fish tank today, and none of the boats were out fishing. Isaac had been loafing around the house, and decided to go out to the benches and see if anyone came by to chat. He had no more than stepped outside when he saw Edfu across the street. He had been thinking about him. His demeanor had always been happy and positive, but lately he seemed down. Isaac suspected he needed something to do; something to make his presence worthwhile. Right now he was scratching Plato behind the ears and talking to him. Isaac wished he could hear the one sided conversation. So, he took a walk across the street.

Edfu heard him coming and turned to see him just as he approached. He flashed a big smile at Isaac and said, "Hello my friend. You are not working today?"

"No. The fish market is not taking any fish today so we have the day off. Who is your friend here that you are talking to?"

"This is Plato; everyone's friend. However, I have heard that he doesn't like bad men."

"True," said Isaac. "Plato seems to live by the adage, 'work hard, play hard, and be kind to others.' I have never seen him balk at work, is always gentle, and I assure you he doesn't like bad guys. While we are talking about Plato, have you taken a look at his harness lately?"

"Yes," replied Edfu. I have noticed that the leather is old and starting to crack in several places. If he is taken on a trip, it could break and leave you to mend it as best you could to get him home."

"That is what I have thought," said Isaac. "Would you consider taking his old harness to the cobbler's shop, and see if you and Abe could design and build him a new one? I will give you the money to pay Abe for his services."

"Surely," said Edfu. I'll start on it right now."

With that, Edfu walked over to Plato's little shed, took the harness off of the wall, threw it over his shoulder, gave Isaac a smile, and started walking toward the cobbler's shop.

As he was walking away, Isaac could hear him singing one of his African songs that he used to hear him sing in the desert. He smiled to himself, thinking, "You did well, Isaac. From now on you need to start using Edfu for jobs around our home. When he finishes this job, we need to gather some fire wood, no one has taken care of the garden since Mother Ruth died, there are some doors that need repair, and the place would look a lot better if we kept the weeds down. Edfu needs to be delegated to be our maintenance man."

Isaac crossed the street and went back in the house.

"When are you going back to work?" Eva asked, as he entered the house.

"David and I have been working the men pretty hard for this past month." he answered. "We decided to take the rest of the week off. There are only two more days."

"Good. We need to stock up on firewood before cool weather sets in." she said. "We can take Ruth, Martha, Mary, the dog, and the kids, and get about three cart loads tomorrow."

Isaac said, "Fine, but we will have to make it the next day. Edfu is making new harness for Plato and it won't be ready by tomorrow morning. I'll check with him to make sure it will be done."

The next day Edfu worked at the forge hammering out iron just as he had done many times making nails for Daniel, except this time he was making a round pin about four times the size of a nail. It had to be smooth with a loop handle on one end.

After studying the harness a little, Edfu decided it could be improved. Now Edfu had a little experience in leatherwork and harness building. During all those years as a camel driver he had made and repaired many camel harnesses. He could redesign Plato's harness a little and make it stronger and much easier to get off and on. After building the new harness with his modifications, he returned home, took Plato to the cart and put the harness on him. But, instead of latching the front and chest straps the way it had been before, he used the pin to go through some loops that Abe had made for him. After it was all together Edfu pulled the pin. When it popped out, the harness fell slack and the shafts dropped on the ground.

It was finished. Edfu was thinking about how the donkey took care of his family, and how they were sometimes so dependent on him. He guessed it was because Plato had been with the family since he was a colt. Starting with Eva he had always been pampered and petted. Everyone in the family had treated him like a member. He accepted new people into the circle of family and all of the children had learned to ride him, talked to him, petted him and fed him treats. When Nikos and Eva moved to Capernaum Plato was their family donkey, but primarily Eva's pet. In his life he had had his neck hugged many times. Plato was a very special little donkey.

Edfu wanted to show the harness off to Eva, since he was her donkey. When she saw Plato in his harness she said, "He looks younger, and look how he walks with his head just a little higher." She said, "Edfu, Plato walks like a man with a new suit. He really likes his new harness. In the morning, most of the family is going on a wood gathering trip. You will have to show us how to hitch him to the cart."

Edfu said, "Even better. I will go with you."

In the morning Edfu was waiting with Plato by his cart. When everyone was there, Edfu held up the new harness and flamboyantly announced that it was a newly developed harness, easy to put on and even easier to take off. With that, he laid the harness over Plato's back, pulled the front strap around, the shoulder strap across, and inserted the pin. "That is it," said Edfu. "It is on."

Then Edfu reached his right hand over to the cart and pulled the pin. The shafts fell to the ground and Edfu shouted, "Hey." Plato quickly stepped out of his harness and Edfu laughed as he said, "You know what he would do now if there were robbers coming at us.

Everyone applauded although the men were a little skeptical of how dependable this army of Edfu and Plato would be. If they did meet some bad guys on the road, Plato had proven himself to be quite a family defender, but they were putting the safety of their family in the hands, so to speak, of a little donkey. Good common sense was still their main defense but they had to admit, it was good to have him around when danger arose.

Isaac said, "Edfu, I want to thank you for all you have put into this and I hope we never need to use it, but if we do I have faith that it will be a great aid to us. Even if we never need it for battle it will last a long time and Plato seems to like it. Now then, our job for today is to gather firewood."

Up the mountain they went, past the point where they usually went for firewood, and then Isaac turned the cart around and stopped. He said, "We will fill the cart up going down the mountain so we won't have to pull a load going uphill."

The children tried to carry too much wood and had to have help getting it in the cart. Buff ran around barking and getting in the way, and for the most part it was more of a party for the children and their dog than a firewood gathering trip. They did get the cart full and back home without incident, except for taking about twice as long as two good men could have done it. When they reached home and had the cart unloaded, Isaac went with Edfu to unhook the cart and put Plato in his pen.

As they walked back to the house Isaac said, "We still need about two more cart loads of wood to last through cold weather. Tomorrow, you and I will go up and get it. The women and children can stay home."

As they walked along, Edfu grinned and said, "Today was fun, but if we had had this group along with us in the wilderness we would have all died the first week."

"Yes," said Isaac. "Yes indeed."

23

LOSS AND DECISIONS

When Timothy and Ruth were married they agreed they would have a large family. Both of them loved children and had always thought, "The more the merrier." But things weren't working out for them. In the first two years of marriage Ruth had lost two children early in her pregnancy. This was their third chance and she was in her eighth month. But, again fate dealt them a hard blow. She went into labor early and the baby was still born. She was small but beautifully shaped and appeared to be a perfect baby, but for some reason died before she had a chance at life.

The whole family was crushed by the loss of the baby, and then for some unknown reason Martha died in her sleep. It was the worst day in the life of the whole family. Martha was the love of Alph's life. In fact, there was no one who didn't love Martha. She was kind, gentle, loving, a good mother and the list of her qualities could fill a book. Alph and the girls, now twelve years old, were lost. The three of them were together constantly as if they were separated for a minute one of them would be gone. Then slowly they began to get their lives reorganized. The girls began to spend more time with Ruth and Grandmother. They cooked the family meals and tried to do everything they had seen their mother do. They took special care of Alph and he loved them dearly.

When he was away from home nothing interested him and he didn't know what to do with himself. For a while the wood working he loved so much didn't seem to mean anything to him. Then one day Atticus sent word to Alph that he had a special desk he wanted him to come up to the barracks and look at. He wasn't going to be moving after all and could make Capernaum home for a while. Alph took a walk, if for nothing else than to just to get away from family, friends and work. When he reached the barracks he was shown to Atticus' office and saw why Atticus wanted him to look at it. It was a huge, beautiful desk, well built, with a thick top and five drawers. But the finish on it was rough and Atticus would like to have it smooth and shiny. Could Alph do anything with it? Alph said it could be finished to any degree Atticus wanted. It would just be a lot of labor. The better the finish, the more hand rubbing it would take, and the labor would determine the cost. Atticus laughed and said, "No problem," Rome had lots of money for improvements.

The truth was, Simon and Atticus had been talking, and Atticus would like to have his desk refinished but what they were really looking for was a simple time consuming job, one that took a lot of hard work and would give Alph time to think while he worked. If Alph could get into something like this, the time alone while he was working just might put a new spark in his life. What they thought he needed was a job where he wouldn't have to think, or measure or plan; just a simple time consuming job with a lot of time to think while he worked.

While all of the events of the past couple of years have been going on, Simon and Mary's son John has grown into a young man. Last week was his Bar Mitzvah and now he has announced that he wants to become a carpenter. These things have been quiet and low key, mostly because of the death of his Aunt Martha, but

Simon and Mary were proud of him, with good reason. He had grown into a fine young man.

Atticus had some soldiers load the desk on a cart and deliver it to the wood shop. Alph took some very fine sand and a very flat piece of sand stone and started rubbing. As he rubbed the surface it began to slowly wear down and the deep scratches and the grooves began to disappear, but it took a lot of rubbing for it to become flat and smooth. By the end of the first day Alph looked at his work and could tell he was a long way from the fine finish Atticus wanted. The next step after many days of rubbing, was to graduate to a pumice stone, rubbing until all the fine scratches from the sand rubbing were gone. After the pumice rub was finished and the desk top was as smooth as he could make it he took a piece of sheep skin. By rubbing with the leather side down the lanolin oil from the skin began to penetrate the wood. Then he turned the wool side down and buffed until the top shined like a mirror. Alph worked on the desk for more than a week, rubbing until his hands and shoulders ached but he didn't have to think much about the work and went over and over in his mind what his life was going to be.

How was he going to raise the girls by himself? Who was going to teach them the woman's things that Martha would have taught them? Part of the time Alph thought about Jesus, about the things he taught, the miracles he performed and the people he healed. Jesus had made his home in Capernaum and Alph had heard his teaching and preaching many times. He also knew that Jesus was not too happy with many of the Capernaum residents, that although they saw and heard, their believing was weak. But, his believing was not weak and neither was the believing of his friends and family. Alph had the feeling that carpentry, as much as he loved it, was no longer what he wanted his number one vocation to be. He wished he had been with Jesus during his ministry in the southern part of the kingdom. He could have learned much more. The man Jesus was the Christ, the Messiah, the son of God, born to an earthly woman but the son of God. So many people missed the whole point. They needed to be told. They needed to be taught.

Where could Alph go to learn more about Jesus? He remembered hearing some men talking about a man named Paul who had been born in Tarsus, became a tent maker, went to school in Jerusalem, was a Pharisee and then became what some were calling a Christian. He was traveling through the gentile area where most of the population was Greek but where many dislocated Jews also lived. He was traveling from city to city teaching Jesus as the Christ, and establishing churches. If only Alph could meet him and learn what he knew, perhaps he could return to Capernaum, and do some of what Jesus did not have time to do. He couldn't perform miracles but he could teach. The Messiah had come, been crucified, dead and buried, rose from the grave, and ascended to heaven. He said he would return, and Alph believed it and thought to himself, "Someone needs to teach this."

The desk was finished and ready to be returned to Atticus. Alph cleaned up his work area and said to Simon "The desk is finished and ready to be returned to the Roman Barracks. I will speak to Edfu and see if he will accompany me on the trip."

Simon said, "You might take John along. If Atticus doesn't have any men handy you will need another strong back to unload it. Atticus should be proud of what you have done. We have never made any fine furniture before but that desk certainly does qualify."

Alph said he was through for the day and went straight to Ruth's house. She and the girls were preparing dinner and having a good time. They were three young girls playing while they worked. It made him feel good to see how well they were doing. Alph knew he needed to pull himself together and decide what he must do with the rest of his life. Miriam took one look at him and said, "Papa you look so tired and sad all the time. I wish we could do something for you."

Maria said, "Papa, we all miss mother but it has been four months now and we want you to be our happy papa. We should remember her with joy and how we all loved one another. Mother wouldn't be happy to know that you were going to be sad forever."

Alph smiled and said, "When did my girls grow up and become so wise." He washed his hands and when they sat down to dinner he asked Timothy if he could offer the prayer.

Then Timothy gave thanks for their wives and mothers and prayed that they might use what they had given them to make good lives for their families, and when he had blessed the food everyone said, "AMEN."

The next morning Alph asked Edfu if he would help haul the desk up to the barracks and Edfu just said, "Let's go."

It was a cool morning and Plato seemed eager to get into harness when he saw them getting the cart ready. Edfu checked over his new special harness and said he thought it all looked good. They took Plato and the cart to the wood shop and with a couple of grunts and a little shove the desk was in the cart but with no room to spare. Alph said he didn't think Plato would have a problem. It was a little uphill most of the way but there were no steep places and they would stop and let him rest once in a while.

After about a half hour of travel they only lacked a few minutes of being to the barracks. As they came around a curve in the road four men came out of the woods and raised their hands. Alph asked, "Can we help you gentlemen?"

One of them said, "Yes. You can help us by walking on up the road and leaving us your donkey, cart, and that lovely desk."

Alph couldn't believe what was happening. There had been no reports of robbers in months and this was happening almost at the Roman Army Barracks. He looked the man straight in the eye and said, "I am afraid we can't do that. We are delivering this desk to the centurion at the barracks."

The man said, "Well I guess we will just have to take it. There's four of us against you, an old man and a boy. I don't think that's a problem." With that the man hit Alph a hard blow to the front of his chest.

Alph is a good sized man, mostly muscle from hard work and usually good natured and easy to get along with, but this wasn't a good time. All of the anger, loss, disappointment and grief had built up inside of him since Martha's death. He drew back and swung a blow with everything in him, hitting the man with his fist right on his nose. The man went backward and landed in a sitting position holding his nose with blood all over him. The other three men started toward Alph but Plato had been prancing in place since the first blow that the man struck and Edfu had already pulled the pin. Plato didn't wait for the HEY command. He was already out of the harness and headed straight for the three men. He hit all three of them going a little bit sideways and sent them sprawling. Plato had already spun around and had started kicking when Edfu got a hold of his bridal. He was afraid that Plato might kill them. One of the men held up his hands and was screaming for them to hold that donkey. They started up the road with the one man holding his nose, one bent over, and one limping badly from the kicks Plato got in before Edfu could get him stopped.

It took a few minutes to get the little donkey settled down. He wanted to go after the men but as soon as they were out of site he stopped tugging for Edfu to let him go, and started braying. Maybe it was a warning to the men or maybe it was his victory song but when he got quiet he was ready to be re-harnessed.

When they reached the Barracks Atticus was standing on the porch talking to the four men. When they saw the donkey cart and its crew coming, the four men started running. Atticus asked Alph what in the world was going on. When Alph told him the story he started laughing and said they came to tell him that there were three big mean men and a crazy donkey, and they had attacked them. I am going to send some men after them. I think the one man may have a broken leg from a donkey kick. If I don't get him for his own good it could be the end of him.

The whole time this was going on John had stood with his mouth open, not saying a word. When they left he finally spoke and said, "Boy do I have a story to tell when we get home, but none of my friends will believe it."

Alph decided that he needed to find Paul and at least talk to him for a while, but what about the girls and the wood shop? The girls must be his first priority. He waited until the girls were out of the house and went to see Ruth. It looks as though she and Timothy are not going to have children and she and the girls have become almost inseparable. Who else could better care for them if he left for a while? He told Ruth what he was thinking but wasn't too sure how long he would be gone, a few months at the least and maybe a year.

Ruth said, "Alph you know that I will take the girls and care for them. Timothy, Mother and Papa will be here to help. You must do what your heart tells you to do."

Alph said, "I thought that was what you would say but I had to ask. Don't say anything to anyone until I have talked to Simon about our shop. Then I will tell the whole family and see what the response is."

Next he went to Simon and explained what he was thinking. He said, "I know this would put a burden on you with all the work we have but I won't leave until you have help."

Simon said, "If this is how you feel you are being led, then this is what you must do. John is learning fast and if I do all the work that is critical he can do well enough on the rest. I have been waiting for you to get back to yourself before we took on any new work. We will make it fine. We just don't need to expand any more right now. And, since you own an interest in the shop I will give Ruth a little each month to help out with the expense of the girls."

Alph also needed to talk to Papa. He walked over toward the fishing dock and saw that Papa's boat was almost unloaded. He waited around until they had finished and Papa was walking up toward home and stopped him in front of the house where they could sit on the benches. He told him the whole story and what he had planned. He said, "Papa this is something that needs to be done and I think I am the one to do it. God hasn't come right out and spoken to me but I feel that he is telling me that this should be my new career. If he wasn't I think he would give me a message to stop before I started."

Isaac said, "Son, if you feel it this strongly then that may be God calling you to do his work. You have my blessing no matter what you do." With that he gave his son a smile and a hug and they each went home.

It had gotten common for the entire family to get together each Sabbath to eat, rest and give thanks for the past week. Mother, Ruth, Mary, Miriam and Marie prepared the food the day before and they had their own Sabbath meal before the sun-set that started the Sabbath. This week, after they had finished eating Alph explained to everyone what he was going to do and that Marie and Miriam would be in the care of Ruth and Timothy while he was gone. The entire family gave him their blessing and he prepared to leave on the first day of the week. Edfu told him to be careful on the road. Plato would not be along to watch out for him. Papa gave him his money belt to wear under his clothes and he was on his way.

For three weeks Alph walked from city to city asking in syna-gogues and of other travelers, "Have you seen or heard of a man of God named Paul." But no one had. One day, in the late afternoon, about half way between Antioch and Laodicea, he topped a small hill and saw three men walking ahead of him, at a much slower gate. One appeared to be crippled.

Alph greeted the men but before he could ask his question the crippled man, who seemed a bit older than the others asked, "Where are you from?"

"I am from Capernaum in Galilee," He said. "And where may you be from?"

"The man answered, "From Tarsus and Jerusalem."

But again before he could ask his question the same man said, "We are about to stop under that tree up ahead, to rest and have some dried fish. We have plenty. Won't you join us?"

Alph said he would, and then decided he would have a chance later to ask his question.

They talked of this and that and the stories came around to times when their inexperience had gotten them in trouble. The older man told of a time when he had agreed to make a tent for a man. He said, "The man wanted the tent long and narrow, so when I put in the flap for a door I put it the middle of one of the long sides. When the man came to get it he said it wasn't what he wanted. He wanted the entrance in one of the ends. So, I stitched up the door flap I had made and put another where he wanted it. When the man came to get it this time he said, "That looks terrible. You should have put a new side in the tent instead of that stitched up door flap." By now I already had more invested in the tent than I was going to get out of it and I just gave it to him to get rid of it. Then he said, "My father teased me about it until the day he died."

Alph related the story of the sand box he made for his girls and John. He said, "I ended up getting myself and my brother-in-law in trouble with our wives and my father still brings it up when he wants a laugh at my expense."

The men asked Alph why he was traveling and he told them that he had heard a man named John speak, who was called the Baptist, and was preaching repentance on the Jordan River and baptizing people for the remission of their sins. He said, "My father and I were baptized by him and witnessed a man named Jesus being baptized. I am sure he was the Messiah, for when he came up out of the water a voice from Heaven said for all of us to hear, "This is my son in whom I am well pleased.' I heard him preach on the mountain, several times in Capernaum where I live, and have witnessed several of his miracles and healings. Jesus is the Christ, and I am looking for a man named Paul to learn more of him that I might preach and teach."

As soon as Alph said this, the men's faces lit up and before he could say more they got to their feet and the older man said, "We have never introduced ourselves. I think we have a lot of talking to do. My name is Paul."

The End

The story you have just read is fiction based on truth. Scripture references are quoted, the places are real, and the book is as historically accurate as possible.

I hope you have enjoyed Alph.
Lee Carson

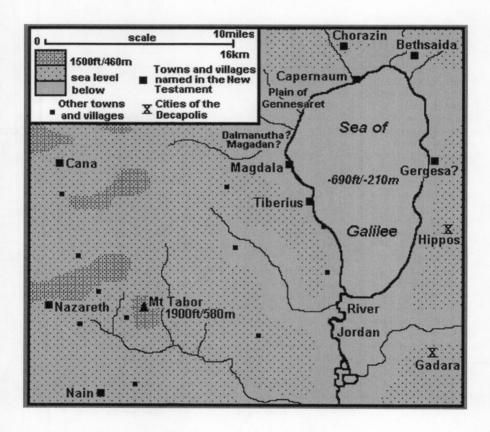

The Sea of Galilee showing the main cities and villages of the area, the Jordan river and elevations above and below sea level.

Made in the USA
Charleston, SC
12 April 2014